AN ALL-AMERICAN GIRL

AN ALL-AMERICAN GIRL

HOWARD RICHARDSON

TATE PUBLISHING
AND ENTERPRISES, LLC

An All-American Girl
Copyright © 2016 by Howard Richardson. All rights reserved.

No part of this publication may be reproduced, stored in a retrieval system or transmitted in any way by any means, electronic, mechanical, photocopy, recording or otherwise without the prior permission of the author except as provided by USA copyright law.

This novel is a work of fiction. Names, descriptions, entities, and incidents included in the story are products of the author's imagination. Any resemblance to actual persons, events, and entities is entirely coincidental.

The opinions expressed by the author are not necessarily those of Tate Publishing, LLC.

Published by Tate Publishing & Enterprises, LLC
127 E. Trade Center Terrace | Mustang, Oklahoma 73064 USA
1.888.361.9473 | www.tatepublishing.com

Tate Publishing is committed to excellence in the publishing industry. The company reflects the philosophy established by the founders, based on Psalm 68:11,

"The Lord gave the word and great was the company of those who published it."

Book design copyright © 2016 by Tate Publishing, LLC. All rights reserved.
Cover design by Samson Lim
Interior design by Manolito Bastasa

Published in the United States of America

ISBN: 978-1-68270-783-8
1. Fiction / Thrillers / Crime
2. Fiction / Mystery & Detective / Police Procedural
16.03.02

This book is dedicated to all those parents who have lost a child due to their getting involved with the wrong crowd of people, so to speak. My children, just like a lot of other parents' children, gave me clues that they were in trouble, but I chose to believe everything was fine. When they were crying out for me to help them, I was so busy in my own life I didn't pick up on any of their signals. I beg each of you reading this book to never get so busy in your life or so intent with making so much money you forget you're their parents, and you need to spend as much time with your children as you can possibly afford while they are reaching out to you for your guidance.

The time to get to know your kids is when they are young, and they need you since when they become grown-ups, in a lot of cases, they too are so busy with their perfect life they don't have time for you either. I miss seeing my grandkids during the time they were growing up, but due to my relationship with my daughter, she does not allow my wife and I to see them. My son will always be in my thoughts and prayers. Daniel is a grown man now and we enjoy spending time with him every chance we get.

My advice is to judge your own life and not the lives of your kids. Be safe and God bless. Thank you for reading my book, and I hope you enjoy it.

DETECTIVE JACK WILLIAMS is a twenty-eight-year-old single man, five feet ten inches tall, with blue eyes, dark hair, a muscular build, and a very nice smile. Jack is a sharp dresser, usually wearing a name-brand sport coat with slacks. Jack's shoes are always shined like new money. He grew up in the town of King, NC, where he was a football star in high school and was very popular with the ladies. Jack was growing up in the Boy Scouts and had lots of friends. Jack was raised by his mom, Linda, and his grandparents on Linda's side of the family, Tony and Maria. He also had a stepdad, Ken Taylor, whom he admired very much in his life while growing up. Ken had his own auto repair business and filled a void in Jack's life since his biological father was not in his life.

Jack was a great student in school and always made wonderful grades. He was taught to do the right thing in any situation and was the good guy. Jack was always commenting to his mom when it came to bullies in school and how unfair it was for them to pick on other students. Jack did not like watching news stories where a human or animal was picked on or harmed by another person for any reason. For this reason, he decided early on in his life he wanted to have a job where his presence made a difference and dedicated his life to helping others. He graduated in the top of his class from the police academy and trained hard for five years until he became a detective.

Jack still lives in King in a modest home and loves to go to the local diner where he ate when he was growing up and where his mother worked. Today, when Jack walks into the diner, everyone knows him, and he speaks to each person there. Jack is the kind of person who, even though he is a detective, lights up the room. Jack is the true definition of the phrase, "Hometown boy does well for himself." He is a well-respected citizen of the town, a member of the local church, and always has a smile on his face.

Allison Tuttle, who lives in a nearby town, Rural Hall, NC, is a very thin sixteen-year-old blue-eyed, blonde-haired athletic cheerleader who seems to have the perfect life. Allison and her family live in a very affluent neighborhood that has decorative street lamps and massive homes. Allison is liked by everyone at Reagan High School, and all of the boys want to be with her. She has lots of friends in school, as well as, I'm sure you can imagine, on the football team and other sports teams. Allison has perfect teeth and a vibrant white smile. She, like most other teenagers, likes to post things on various social media sites.

Allison has had boyfriends in school but has not yet found someone who she feels is popular enough and good-looking enough for her. All of her classmates think she is spoiled by her parents, but each one of them would trade places with her in a minute. She loves her life but wants so much more out of her future. Allison's family is good friends with Detective Jack William's family and Jack as well. Allison's dad, Paul Tuttle, is a pillar of the community since he is a well-liked pastor at the local church. Paul wants nothing but the best for his family and raises his children to live a Christian lifestyle. Allison's mom, Jennifer Tuttle, a very pretty blonde in her own right, works for a local insurance company and is an active member with the PTA. Allison has an older brother, Landon Tuttle, twenty-three, who, like most older brothers, wants to protect his sister as well as be her friend. She also has a younger sister, Lisa Tuttle, thirteen, who is not as popular or as pretty as Allison but tries very much to be like her sister.

Allison's best friend in school for eight years is Heather, who is a bright young girl that secretly resents Allison's popularity and looks. She is also sixteen and a pretty girl but does not get near the praise Allison has gotten all these years. Heather makes better grades than Allison and even helps her academically when she needs answers to questions or quizzes. Since Allison's dad bought her a brand new car for her sixteenth birthday, she now works part-time at a local restaurant/diner as a waitress and loves the attention she gets from her customers.

On Tuesday, September 10, Detective Jack found himself near the restaurant where Allison was working, so he decided to stop in. He entered the restaurant and noticed Allison immediately and asked to be seated at one of her tables. Allison went over to Jack, and the two of them exchanged greetings. Jack commented on how much Allison has grown and told her how pretty she has gotten. Allison told Jack she was told he was now a detective, and she congratulated him on his position. Allison flashed Jack the million-dollar smile and took his order.

While Allison was gone, Jack overheard a conversation between two of the other waitresses and hears one of them say, "Look how she's dressed like the slut she is. No wonder she gets away with it since she's banging the boss." Jack also noticed Allison was wearing a dress that was shorter than the other waitresses' and was wearing lots of makeup. When Allison returned with Jack's food, he notices she is wearing some very expensive diamond earrings and tells her she must be doing really well at her job. Allison tells him the tips are very good, and she loves interacting with the public.

Before Jack got ready to pay his bill and leave, he noticed one of the restaurant's busboys and Allison exchanging words. He knew he had seen this busboy somewhere but couldn't remember where. Jack asked if everything is all right, and the busboy tells him everything is fine with "Miss Prissy." Jack asked Allison if the boss is good to work with, and she said he's all right, but he needs to keep his hands to himself. Jack then paid his bill and told Allison that if she is having problems with these guys, she needs to tell him, but she dismissed it as no big deal. Allison said, "I can take care of myself, but thanks." Detective Jack left her his card and told her if she ever needs anything to please call him. Allison stuck the card Jack gave her in her apron but pretty much dismissed the whole incident.

Later that same day, Detective Jack ran into Allison's mom, Jennifer, at the grocery store where she was buying groceries for the week. Jack told Jennifer he saw Allison at the restaurant where she was working. He asked her if everything is all right with the family and with Allison. She said everything is fine with Landon, Lisa, and Paul. She stated Allison loves working at the restaurant but complained the tips were not that great. Jack mentioned he noticed the expensive diamond earrings Allison was wearing and wondered if they were a birthday present. Jennifer stated she did not think she had seen them, but she was sure they weren't a birthday present since Allison had just gotten a new car. She told Jack that perhaps Allison had borrowed them from her jewelry box.

Jack described the earrings, and Jennifer stated she did not have any earrings that shape. He also asked if she knew the name of the busboy working at the restaurant, and she told him, "No, why do you ask?" Jack just simply told her he thought he knew that guy from someplace else. He asked Jennifer if she knew where the boy lived, and she stated she did not. Jennifer could see Jack recognized the guy from somewhere and started to grow concerned for Allison's safety.

When Jack got back to his office, he started looking at the mug shot books, which are books used to find people who have been arrested with photos taken of these individuals, to see if he could spot the busboy he had seen at the restaurant. After looking through the books for an hour or so, he did not find the individual he had seen. Jack asked the sheriff deputies in the building at the time if they had seen this busboy, but no one could place his face anywhere except the restaurant. It continued to bother Jack for some time after that since he was sure he had seen the busboy somewhere before but could not place him.

An All-American Girl

When Allison's mom got home from the grocery store, she remembered what Jack had told her regarding the earrings he saw on Allison at the restaurant. Allison's mom started looking through her jewelry box, but all of her jewelry was accounted for. She kept wondering where Allison could have come up with the money for the expensive diamond earrings.

When Allison's dad, Paul, came home, Jennifer told him she had seen Detective Jack that afternoon at the grocery store, and she also told him the story Jack had told her regarding the earrings. She asked Paul if he had bought the expensive earrings, and he told her he had no idea what she was talking about.

When Allison came home from work that evening, Jennifer asked her how her day went at work. Allison did not even mention she had seen Detective Jack at all. Then Allison's dad came into the room and asked her if she remembered seeing Jack at the restaurant, and she replied, "Oh yeah, he stopped by. How did you know he was there?"

Paul stated Jack had run into her mom at the grocery store, then he asked her how were her tips for the day. Allison stated, "The tips are always bad on this job. I need to find something where I can make more money." Paul noticed she did not have on any earrings and asked her where the earrings were that she had on at the restaurant.

Allison asked how he knew about it, and Paul just said, "Jack mentioned you had them on when he saw you."

Allison stated they belonged to one of her friends, and that friend had come by the restaurant to pick them up before she got off work.

Paul asked her, "Why would you have been wearing them if they belonged to someone else?"

Allison replied, "I knew if I had them on no one could steal them out of my purse."

Even though this whole story didn't make sense to either Allison's dad or mom, they just let the issue drop.

Before Allison went to bed, her mom came into her room and asked if everything was all right with her at the restaurant, and she told her mom, "Everything's fine."

Jennifer asked about the busboy Jack had asked about.

"Mom, he's just some loser who was hired by Chuck, my boss. I can handle my own self."

Jennifer asked her daughter if the guy was giving her any trouble, and all Allison would say was, "I'm a big girl, and I can handle him."

Allison then told her mom she was very tired and wanted to go to sleep. Jennifer told her if she ever has anyone like this guy bothering her to please let someone know. Then Jennifer left the room.

When Jennifer went back into the living room, she and Paul started talking about what had happened and what

An All-American Girl

Jack had said. She told Paul she believed their daughter and thought it was a great idea to have the expensive earrings on instead of having them in her purse where someone could have stolen them. Paul stated he was unsure of Allison's story, but he wanted to believe his daughter would do the right thing in this situation, and he trusted her. As Jennifer and Paul were watching television before retiring for the evening, as they did every evening, neither one of them brought up the subject, yet there was a strong feeling of uneasiness in the air.

On Wednesday morning, when Allison came down for breakfast, her mom and dad were there and once again told her how proud they were of her for handling the earring situation the way she did. Paul also told her he wanted her to know that he was a busy man but never too busy to help her if she needed it. Allison advised both her parents that she was fine and did not need their help; but if she did, she would let them know. After Allison had eaten her half of a grapefruit before leaving for school, she kissed her parents and headed off for a long day at school. She also told her parents she had to work tonight even though she was not on the schedule as she was filling in for someone else. They agreed, and she left the house.

Once Allison got to her school, she found her group of friends and advised them if her mom were to call any of them asking about some expensive diamond earrings to tell her she had borrowed the earrings from them. Allison began laughing and joking with her friends like she does every day at school. Allison and her friends started walking to class when Michael, a former boyfriend of Allison's, came by and asked her if she wanted to go out one night on the weekend.

Allison responded by saying, "I would rather date an animal than go out with you."

Michael was very offended and yelled back at Allison, "One of these days you'll be sorry for the way you treat me."

Allison just laughed it off as she and her friends walked away.

Allison and Heather were in the same math class together, and on this day the teacher decided to give the class a pop quiz, which, of course, Allison was not even close to being ready for. The math teacher handed out the test when Allison told her teacher she was feeling ill and needed to go to the nurse's office. The math teacher reluctantly gave Allison a hall pass to go see the nurse. Allison arrived at the nurse's office only to find the nurse had stepped out. But instead of Allison returning to her math class, she went to her locker, removed her books, and left the school.

Later that same day, Allison did show up for work at the restaurant but was not wearing the same clothes she had been wearing when she left her house in the morning. When Allison left her home for school, she was wearing whitewashed jeans, a clingy red crop top, and white sneakers. When she arrived at work, she was wearing her work clothes, which consisted of her work dress and her black sneakers. Had Allison gone home from school and changed clothes? Where else would she have gotten her work clothes? Allison was also wearing the expensive diamond earrings again.

While Allison was working her shift at the restaurant, a man came in, a man no one was familiar with, except Allison. One patron overheard her call the man Fred. She was very friendly toward Fred, and several times during Fred's time in the restaurant, she could be heard giggling over things he would say to her.

Chuck, Allison's boss, came over during one of the giggling sessions and told her, "I pay you to work not to giggle."

Allison responded to Chuck, "You pay me to bring business into your restaurant and to be extra friendly to your customers, which I do. You're just pissed off because I won't giggle with you. You're a pervert. I see you checking out my ass when I bend over a table, and you love it."

The patrons in the restaurant were shocked to hear Allison speak this way and also to learn Chuck might be trying to hit on Allison. Chuck is a middle-aged man who is old enough to have children, Allison's age, let alone try to hit on the high school cheerleader. Chuck finally went back to what he was doing and left Allison alone to do her job. After a few more minutes, the man known as Fred paid his bill, left the restaurant, and drove away. Allison never said anything to any of the patrons as to how she knew this man or where she knew him from.

When she finished her shift at the restaurant and was preparing to go home, she was surprised to see her brother Landon pull up in his vehicle and come inside. Landon came in and gave his sister a big hug and a kiss on the cheek. Allison was shocked to see Landon there this late. She asked him why did he come by so late?

Landon responded he had not seen her in a while and just thought he'd come by and escort her home.

Allison thanked her brother but was very reluctant to let him escort her home. She said she was going to stop off at a friend's house, but she would just do that tomorrow. Allison and Landon left the restaurant in separate vehicles and headed to their parents' house.

When they arrived, they both went inside to find their parents waiting for what they assumed would just be Allison coming home as always. Paul, Jennifer, and Lisa, the younger sister, welcomed both Allison and Landon with open arms. The whole family visited for a short time before Lisa had to go to bed and Landon had to go home to his apartment in Winston-Salem. A few minutes later, Allison was off to bed.

After Allison had gone to bed, Landon called his mother to tell her he did not see any diamond earrings on Allison when he got to the restaurant. He went on to say he did not see any wrongdoings while he was at the restaurant either from the busboy or the owner. Landon, of course, was unaware that Fred had come by the restaurant, so he had no information regarding that. He did comment on Allison's clothing and her dress being so short. He told his mother that he did not think it was something a sixteen-year-old girl should be wearing. When Jennifer got off the phone, she asked Paul about the information Landon had just given her. Paul told Jennifer he had asked Landon to go by and check on Allison since he was not convinced she was telling the truth, and he would feel better if he knew for sure. Paul stated he was the pastor in this town and could not let some rumor regarding his daughter get blown out of proportion. Jennifer was not very happy that Paul had done this behind her back. She told him they were in this marriage together, and he had no right to have anyone spy on their children. Finally, the couple turned in for the evening.

On Thursday morning, Allison came down to the breakfast table, ate her half of grapefruit, and left for school. When she got to school and went through her usual routine with her friends, her first class was math. When she arrived at the math class, her teacher was waiting for her. The teacher asked Allison what happened to her yesterday when she went to the nurse's office. Allison started crying and told the teacher the nurse was gone, so she felt so bad she just left and went home to rest. Since Allison's grades were always above par, the teacher felt sorry for her and let her take the pop quiz she missed in class from the previous day. Allison was able to pass the test by getting some of the answers from Heather.

Once the math class was over, Heather confronted Allison in the hall and told her she was tired of having to bail her out by giving her the answers. Heather went on to say she was also tired of being treated like she was beneath Allison. She told her that she was on her own, and she would no longer bail her out. Allison shouted at Heather, telling her she was not worried, that she would be back. Allison went to her next class like nothing had happened.

When Allison got out of class, Heather was there waiting for her.

Allison said, "I told you you'd be back."

Heather told her, "You'll treat me better, or I'll tell your mom where you got the diamond earrings you were wearing."

"You wouldn't dare."

"Not only that, I'll tell her everything, and you know I know all about your little activities."

Allison was so mad at Heather but had no choice except to agree since she knew Heather could ruin everything for her. Allison's perfect little world was starting to crumble right before her eyes. She did the only thing she could think of: she grabbed Heather and hugged her while sobbing. Allison kept telling Heather she was her best friend, and she would always be her best friend. Heather pretended to go along, but she knew this was all a part of who Allison was.

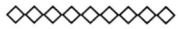

When Allison got out of school that day, there was a man waiting at her car. The man looked like someone you might like to avoid in a dark alley. Heather, Allison, and a few other girls were walking toward the parking lot when they asked Allison if she knew the man, and Allison stated she knew him and she would see the other girls tomorrow. Allison started walking toward the car as the other girls just stood there watching her get closer to the man. The girls were shocked when they saw Allison speak to the man and then got into her car and drove off. The girls were worried when they saw the man drive off right behind Allison.

That evening Allison was on social media when Heather saw her online. Heather asked Allison who the guy was from the school parking lot.

Allison replied, "He is helping me get more exposure on my website."

Heather asked Allison what website she was talking about.

Allison responded, "I want to have fun, so I decided to post pictures of myself having fun."

Heather asked if she thought that was safe.

"No one will even know except the people who subscribe to the website."

She asked Allison about her parents finding out and Allison replied, "My family won't be asked to join the website, so they'll never know."

"Why would you do this?"

"It makes me extra money. He's already helping me make money, so why not. It's all in good fun. You should try it."

"No way." Then Heather asked Allison what she was going to be doing on the website.

"Just wearing bathing suits and special underwear."

"Who is doing the pictures and the video?"

Allison told Heather the guy from the parking lot, Adam, the photographer and the one posting the website. Heather asked Allison if she was having sex with this guy.

Allison said, "He's tried, but I have him right where I want him."

"That's a dangerous game you're playing. What if he forces you?"

"Don't worry about me. I like the attention. I can take care of myself."

Heather then replied, "It's your life. Who is going to pay to see you in your underwear?"

Allison told Heather that Adam said he had websites with more than a thousand people paying $34.95 a month to see girls in their underwear.

"Must be weirdos and sick bastards."

Allison said, "Hey, as long as these perverts are willing to pay, it's okay with me. It's not like I have to have sex with anyone. It's just role-playing. I pretend like I'm really hot for them, and they get their jollies watching me."

"That's just weird."

Allison said, "Just don't tell anyone about this."

Heather said she wouldn't.

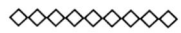

On Friday morning, Allison went through her usual morning routine but as she was getting ready to run out of the door to school, her dad was reading the newspaper. Allison's dad told her a man had been arrested for soliciting sex from teenagers in a city in South Carolina. Allison asked her dad what that had to do with her. Allison's dad just replied, "Allison, I know you think you can do anything you want and no harm will come to you, but it's not as easy as you think."

"Dad, where that happened, that's a long way from here and you worry too much." Allison ran out the door on her way to school.

After Allison left, her dad told Jennifer, "I don't know what I'd do if someone treated my daughter that way. I know I'm a man of God and a God-fearing man, but I just don't know how far away my breaking point would be. God blessed us with three wonderful children, and I can't imagine life without either one of our kids."

Jennifer replied, "Paul, I know you, and I know you would try to forgive the person for being that weak. I also know you're a man and a father first. God would understand."

Allison got to school on time and met with Heather and her friends as always. The bunch of girls gossiped and made comments about other kids as they laughed when kids they didn't associate with walked by. Some of the girls would even call unkind names to the unpopular kids as they walked by. The girls had special names for the students the girls thought were too far beneath them. Finally, the school bell rang, and all of the kids went on to their respective classes.

The football team was playing at home tonight so the school had scheduled a pep rally before the game. At the pep rally, the entire regular click of friends was there along with all of the cheerleaders and, of course, the football team. Allison was in rare form since she was the cheerleader the others threw into the air to do stunts. Before game time, the cheerleaders had a meeting, and the coach advised the cheerleaders a big test was coming up and if anyone on the squad failed the test, they would not be able to compete in the cheerleading contests that were coming up next month. All of the cheerleaders understood the instructions and Allison knew she was safe since Heather was always helping her with her testing.

The game started, and the home team won. After the game, some of the football players and the cheerleaders went to the restaurant/diner where Allison usually worked to get something to eat and drink. When the players and cheerleaders arrived at the restaurant, they packed the place. Chuck came over to Allison and told her she needed to start taking orders from the crowd. Allison told Chuck she was not working right now, that she was a customer. The two of them got into a rather heated discussion right there in front of all those customers.

Chuck told Allison if she won't help them in this crisis, then she is fired. Allison could not afford to get fired until she was able to get another way to make enough money, so she worked in her cheerleading uniform. Her cheerleading uniform was like most any other. The body of the uniform covered most of your torso and then, like panties, covering your bottom. Allison caught Chuck and the busboy both staring at her when she would clean off a table. Allison was mad since she had to work and then to have these creeps staring at her just put her over the top. Allison walked over to the busboy and told him she hated his guts and wished he would get fired. Allison then turned her attention over to her boss and told him she wished his wife would find out about his drooling over her, and she left.

When Allison got home, she came running into the house in tears and told her mom and dad what happened at the restaurant. Allison's dad was furious. and even though he was a pastor, he left going to the restaurant to have a word with Chuck and John. Allison's mom stayed home with Allison to help her calm down and stop crying.

When Paul got to the restaurant, he saw Chuck and John. He walked right up to Chuck and demanded an explanation for his behavior after what he was told by Allison. Chuck told Paul that Allison came into the restaurant, and all these people with her knew Chuck did not have enough help with Allison not working. He claimed he asked Allison to work, and she said she would. He even called John over to confirm this was the correct information. Both Chuck and John agreed it was not anyone's fault the restaurant was so swamped, but Chuck was thankful for the business Allison had brought into the restaurant that night.

Before leaving, Paul asked both men about their behavior toward his daughter staring at her when she had on this skimpy cheerleading uniform. Both men told Paul neither of them were remotely interested in Allison since they knew she was only sixteen years of age. Both men also told Paul that Allison had wished John would get fired from his job, and she had threatened to tell Chuck's wife about his supposedly staring at Allison. Just before Paul left, Chuck mentioned Allison's regular uniform she had been wearing and the shortness of the dress. Chuck told Paul he did not give Allison the dress that short, and Allison had it altered to be that short. Chuck also told Paul that Allison came in to work, wearing all types of makeup and jewelry to make her look sexy to the patrons. Paul was very upset at hearing this news and stormed out of the restaurant. Paul was heard as he left the building saying, "I am not raising a tramp. I refuse to be humiliated by anyone, especially my own daughter."

When Paul got back home, he came into the house, and Jennifer immediately knew something was wrong. Jennifer asked Paul what happened at the restaurant. Paul responded, "We have a problem. Where's Allison?" Jennifer told Paul that Allison went to bed after she finally calmed her down. Jennifer took Paul by the hand and led him into the living room. The couple sat down on their sofa so they could have a conversation. Paul began by telling Jennifer when he had gotten to the restaurant, he confronted Chuck and John. Paul told her Chuck claimed when Allison and the cheerleaders got to the restaurant, Chuck asked Allison to help out, and she said she would. A story completely different than the story Allison had told. Paul went on to say, "That's not all. The dress Allison wears to work was altered to make it shorter by Allison, not by Chuck. Chuck also claims Allison wears lots of makeup to work and jewelry to make her look sexier."

Jennifer said, "That's a lie."

Paul replied, "Chuck and John both claim they have no romantic interest in Allison. Do we even know our own daughter? Could we have been so blind? This scares me to death."

Jennifer said, "Let's sit down with Allison in the morning and sift through these stories until we get some answers."

The couple hug one another unsure of the answers they will get in the morning. They both began crying, not knowing where they may have gone wrong. Were they really that blind about their daughter? They fell asleep on the sofa just holding one another. Jennifer awoke a few hours later and took Paul by the hand and led him off to bed.

On Saturday morning, the couple was up early and was sitting downstairs when Allison came down to the table. Allison looked at her dad and mom and asked, "What's wrong?" Allison's dad told her everything he had told her mom last night. He said he was trying to believe her, but everything she claimed had happened at the restaurant was disputed by Chuck and John. Allison started making excuses for the differences in the two stories until her dad said, "Allison, stop. Let's start with the dress you wear to work. You, not Chuck, had the dress altered to make it shorter."

Allison said, "Dad, you're wrong, and I have to go meet Heather."

"We are not going anywhere except to the restaurant to straighten this whole thing out once and for all. Also, if I find out you lied to me and you did not even have enough respect for me to tell me the truth, I will sell your car and you can ride the bus to school."

Paul, Jennifer, and Allison were getting ready to walk out the door to confront Chuck and John about the lies Allison claimed they told about her, when Allison told her parents she needed to clear up a few things. The family members sat down, and Allison began to tell her story. "Chuck lied about me offering to work at the restaurant last night. I was having a good time with my friends and had no desire to work, but Chuck told me he would pay me overtime if I worked. I hemmed my dress worn at the restaurant since it was longer than the fashions are right now. You know I try to dress up, and I like to look nice, so I paid to have it hemmed. As far as Chuck and John looking at my butt when I lean over to clean a table, to be honest I have gotten used to the customers who looked as well, and for some reason, the ones who do usually leave me a better tip. It's no different than when we go to the beach, and I have on a bikini. You can't see anything. I know that doesn't please you, but that's the truth. Dad, I know you're not proud of me, and I'm sorry to disappoint you. John and Chuck have both come onto me, and I told them I'd call the law if I had to, and I reminded them both I am only sixteen. I'm jail bait. As for the makeup, I like the way it made me look."

Paul and Jennifer both hugged Allison and told her they appreciated her telling them the truth. Paul told Allison, "You did the right thing telling Chuck and John you'd call the law. After all, we know Jack, and he is the law."

Allison then told her parents Jack had given her his card when he was at the restaurant, and she had it in her apron at work. Neither parent brought up the jewelry so Allison did not mention it either. She knew she dodged a bullet by not having to confront Chuck and John since one of them was bound to bring up the jewelry and the diamond earrings. Allison's parents told her they would allow some makeup as long as she looked like a lady instead of a hooker. Paul even offered to have Allison's mom take Allison to the mall and get her makeup professionally done. Everyone seemed to have a weight lifted off their shoulders just to get all this out in the open, or so it seemed.

Paul went to work, and Jennifer took Allison to the mall to get her makeup done professionally as promised by her dad. Before the two ladies headed out for the mall, Allison called Heather and told her she would see her later. While Jennifer and Allison were at the mall, they not only had their makeup done, they also had a manicure and a pedicure.

Before the two ladies left the mall, there was a man Allison noticed standing outside one of the boutiques and who seemed to be watching her. Jennifer asked Allison if she was ready for lunch, and Allison asked if they could go to the local Mexican restaurant. When the two ladies left the Mexican restaurant, Allison noticed the same man from the mall was standing outside, watching the two women as they walked to their car. As Jennifer drove away, Allison kept looking in the mirror to see if the man was following them. After a few minutes had passed, Allison had not seen a vehicle that seemed to be following them, so she stopped looking for the man.

When the two ladies arrived back at the family home, they spent the afternoon talking until Allison told her mom she wanted to go check her e-mails and social media accounts. She went upstairs and got online on her computer and got an e-mail from Adam who had posted a few of Allison's photos wearing all types of outfits to her new website. Allison went into the website and was laughing at some of the silly photos posted but was also intrigued by the ones showing her wearing lingerie. She really thought she looked hot in the shots where she was wearing very sheer lingerie. Allison responded back to Adam she loved the layout and wrote to Heather and gave her the password to sign in to the website. Allison couldn't wait to get men paying to see her tease them. She loved the photos, and the video was incredible, and she felt like she was a movie star.

In the evening, Allison was on the Internet when Heather got online. Heather sent Allison a text saying she had looked at the website and was shocked at some of things she saw on the video. Allison sent a text back saying it was just her having fun and enjoying herself. The two went back and forth, exchanging texts for about an hour when Allison got a text from Adam. Adam asked Allison what she thought of the photos and video. She wrote back saying she loved them, and she couldn't wait until people started watching them. Adam told her he had already sold about a hundred memberships to people all over the country. Allison was excited that people wanted to see her having fun and wearing the underwear. Adam told her if she wanted to go further, she'd have a lot more interest. Allison asked what did he mean, and he wrote back saying that if she wanted to show more of her, like posing topless or having a playmate.

Allison told Adam she was not interested, so Adam wrote her saying the ones with thousands of followers pose topless or nude. Adam went on to say she didn't have to have sex; just more fun posing before the camera. Adam also said he would send Allison a link to a couple other websites so she could see what they do to attract other followers. Allison wrote back that she would take a look at the websites. She got the website passwords from Adam and saw what sells on these. She sent one of the website passwords to Heather. Heather wrote Allison saying she was appalled by the sick things she saw on the website. Allison just said, "You're just jealous because no one wants to see you naked. That's all."

Heather said, "I just don't believe I have to show my ass to the world to be liked."

Allison replied, "Who'd pay to see your ass?"

"You can really be a bitch sometimes, you know. I hope you don't regret showing your ass to some pervert." Heather begged Allison not to get involved with this type of behavior.

Allison wrote back to Adam and said she looked at it, but she couldn't see herself doing anything like that. Adam just wrote back, "I don't want you to do anything you're not comfortable with. But if you want to make more money than you can count, this is the way."

Allison said she just wanted to see where her website goes. Adam told her for one hundred followers on her website, she gets 10 percent. The other girls on the websites he showed her get 20 to 25 percent of one thousand followers at $34.95 per follower monthly. Allison immediately started thinking of all the things she could do with that kind of money.

That night, Allison was lying in bed but couldn't go to sleep for thinking of all the things she wanted in life for she was very impatient to get some of these things. Allison thought to herself who's going to be hurt with this website. It's just people watching other people having fun. Allison also thought if her parents found out what she was doing, they would be devastated. She got up from her bed and wrote to Adam asking him questions like, Who decides who gets a membership? How do you verify someone's identity on the website? How can I be sure none of my family is going to see these photos or video? How can we be sure none of my friends see these photos or video?

Adam wrote back to Allison saying there are no guarantees as to who sees the website, but the viewer does have to put in their credit card number so they know who is buying a membership. Adam promised Allison if her dad or family ever put in their credit card number, he would make sure they were denied access. She told Adam she would think about doing more on the site as long as he promised not to give access to her family. Of course, Adam wrote back, he would make sure anyone with her last name would be denied.

Allison tossed and turned the remainder of the night thinking of all the wonderful things she could buy with the money. She had visions of thousands of followers, and quite honestly, she was starstruck with the possibility of all these people swooning over, seeing Allison having fun. Allison even dreamed of being a film star, showing off her sexy body to the world and getting all the recognition doing it. Allison could picture herself kissing some handsome male movie star and having him hold her close. She began to think about the sex aspects of these people holding her and became aroused. She couldn't help but think one day she would even have a more perfect life by doing these videos.

On Sunday morning, Allison was like most kids, when all they want to do is sleep. But since she is the pastor's daughter, she was expected to get up and get ready for Sunday school and for church. The whole family was up so they could have a family breakfast together like they did every Sunday morning. Paul did most of the cooking on Sunday so as to give Jennifer a day off and he could pamper her some. Paul enlisted his son to help with the cooking duties. Landon had set the table with the Sunday china and put out the linen napkins. Paul and Landon collectively cooked bacon, eggs, gravy, and home-made biscuits.

When breakfast was ready, the family sat down at the dining room table where Paul would say the grace and everyone had to go around the table, telling something good that had happened to them that week. Paul started with God had blessed him with his beautiful family and his graces. Jennifer was next and said she had gotten the chance to spend more time with her kids during the week. Landon said he had gotten a raise at work, and he thought that was a good thing. Allison said she was very proud her school had won the game on Friday and she was happy to be so beautiful. Lisa said she had gotten a really good grade on a project she did for school that week. The family sat and talked about all kinds of subjects and then cleared away the dishes and finished getting ready for church.

After church had let out, the family went to a local restaurant for their Sunday lunch together. Most of the church's congregation went to the same restaurant. Church members came over and shook Paul's hand and spoke to each family member individually. Everyone seemed to enjoy this time together. Once the meal was over, the family went home, and like most families on Sunday got into their relaxing clothing.

Paul and Landon would be in the den to watch some type of sporting event while Jennifer would sit in the living room watching a movie on Lifetime. Allison and Lisa would go upstairs to their separate rooms and play on their computers. At dinner time, they usually had sandwiches and just relaxed until bedtime.

The next Monday morning, Allison barely made it down the stairs to the breakfast table. She looked like she had been up all night. Allison's family all commented on how tired she looked. Lisa was making jokes about her sister talking about how red her eyes were. Allison's mom got some eyedrops for Allison to put in her eyes before leaving for school.

Once the kids were on their way to school, Paul and Jennifer had a chance to talk about the events over the last two days. Jennifer told Paul she appreciated him letting her take Allison to the mall to get their makeup done, as well as the pedicure and manicure. Paul asked if that made Allison feel better, and Jennifer told him she thought that went a long way to mending hurt feelings.

Once Allison got to school, she met with her crew that included Heather and started sharing gossip, as usual. All of the girls noticed Allison's new makeup and manicure and how the two accents made Allison look happy as well as even more beautiful. One of the girls commented on how Allison seemed to be in better spirits than usual and asked her if she had something new going on in her life. All Allison would say was she had a few new things on the horizon and was excited about the possibilities. Heather and Allison agreed to meet after school to talk more about their online conversation. It was just a few minutes later and the bell to go to class went off, and the girls went their separate ways.

When school got out, Heather met Allison at Allison's car. The two girls got into the car and started talking about the website. Some of their friends saw them in the car and came over so Allison excused herself and told her other friends she had to go to work. She told them she was going to drop Heather at her home along the way. Heather and Allison started sharing opinions about the site and the video. Heather tried to convince Allison this was a bad idea, at least in her opinion. Allison tried to convince Heather this was a great opportunity to make great money without getting hurt or hurting others. Heather told Allison she did not know this Adam that well, and of course, he was going to tell her anything she wanted to hear to get her onboard.

Heather told Allison that if someone has a credit card, there is no way they are not going to sign them as a member, no matter what Adam said. Allison tried to defend her position by saying Adam had promised not to let her family get approved as a member. Heather came back with what if that doesn't happen? What if your family sees these photos and video or videos? Allison just said she would have to deal with that if that day ever came. Heather told Allison it was time she starts to think about someone other than Allison. Heather went on to say the whole world does not revolve around Allison and what she wants. Allison got mad, and the two girls had an argument just about the time the car stopped at Heather's house. Heather got out of the car and was still trying to talk to Allison, but Allison just said to Heather, "You wouldn't understand. You've never had to deal with being beautiful and having lots of people want you."

Heather responded, "I may not be as beautiful as you are, but at least I do my own work. I don't depend on others to bail my ass out all the time."

Allison then said, "I don't need your help. I don't need anything from anyone. I can do for myself."

"You're right. You don't need anyone except perverts and weirdos. You're a bitch, and I hope you get what's coming to you."

Heather ran into her house, and Allison sped away.

Allison was so mad when she got to the restaurant to work she was in no mood to take any crap of anyone. John was first in line for the Allison train. John greeted her when she came in the door, "What's up, prissy, hard day at school?"

She looked right at him and said, "I had a great day at school. I got pissed off just knowing I was coming here to work with people like you."

John just said, "What a bitch." And John kept walking.

Allison went in the ladies' room to change into her work outfit. When she came out, she then took her school clothes to her car. She returned from her car and got ready to start her shift. She worked about two hours when she saw Fred come in to the restaurant. Fred sat down at one of her tables, and when Allison came over to take his order, Fred whispered to Allison he had become a member of this website he found on the Internet. Allison froze and had a deer-in-the-headlight look when Fred touched Allison's hand and said, "I loved everything about it." She could not help but smile from ear to ear and then thanked Fred for his comments. Before Fred left the restaurant, he told Allison the site has over one hundred followers, which made Allison very happy. Fred told Allison that if she ever wanted to be even bolder with her site, he could suggest some ideas. Allison did not respond but did smile. The rest of Allison's night went pretty well, and she did notice a couple of people coming into the restaurant she had not seen there before. Allison began to wonder what information was on the website other than just the pictures and the video.

When Allison got home and spoke to her family, she quickly excused herself, saying she was very tired and just wanted to turn in for the night. Allison went upstairs and got on her computer. She saw Adam was online, and she asked him if the people who became members knew anything about her personally. Adam stated some of the members want more information about the participants so they give them the area of the country they are located in. Allison was frantic and asked Adam why would they do such a thing, that she saw a couple of people at the restaurant tonight she had not seen before.

Adam told Allison, "We don't give them the name of the town or where you work or live. If you had new customers, maybe it's just because you are doing a great job there."

Allison then told Adam about Fred, who came in tonight saying he had signed up as a member. Adam was very concerned and cautioned Allison not to get too friendly with Fred since some of these people may not be seeing this as fun. Some of these people may be connected in some way. She asked what he meant by that. He said, "A lot of these guys have business connections with people who produce porn videos, and they look for young women to add to their collection." Adam just replied some of these guys get carried away with their memberships and feel like they have some connection with the girls.

Allison was very nervous and asked Adam if anyone had ever gotten hurt off the website. Adam told Allison there is always a chance some guy will figure out who you are based on information they get from another member. She asked Adam why he did not tell her any of that before she got involved. Adam told her not to worry; he would be very careful what information was released about her since he liked her more than most of the girls. Adam asked Allison if she had thought about posting a more interesting video, but Allison responded she was surprised to actually meet someone who became a member of the website.

Adam calmed her down by saying this was one guy out of thousands who look at these sites, so her chances of being found by someone off the website was very slim. Allison accepted the response and decided she was more afraid of not having money than from these perverts finding out who she is. Allison agreed to meet Adam tomorrow since she was off work to shoot another video.

When Allison awakened Tuesday morning, she bounded down the stairs to see the start of a new day. Allison's parents were very happy to see how energetic she was this morning. Allison's sister asked her if she took some energy drink before coming down stairs. Allison just said she knows today is going to be awesome. Paul and Jennifer encouraged Allison to make this day special. Allison says she knows this will be a day she will never forget. She gobbled down her half grapefruit and told Lisa, "Grab your book bag and let's go." Allison told her mom on the way out she has to work tonight and ran out the door with her little sister in tow. Allison dropped Lisa off at her school and headed to Reagan High School.

Allison arrived at her school to find her friends waiting for her minus Heather. The girls asked her why Heather is not coming over to them. Allison said Heather showed her true colors yesterday, and she wanted nothing else to do with her. Allison began running Heather down just the same way the crew had been doing to others every day. The group saw Heather talking to some of the other girls the cool crew won't have anything to do with. Heather just kept talking to them until the bell rang for all of the students to go to class.

When class was over and Allison was walking toward her car, Michael walked up to Allison and said, "Hey, baby, where you headed?"

Allison told Michael it's none of his business.

Michael said, "Can you drop me off at home?"

Allison told him she is in a hurry, but Michael begged for a ride since he missed his bus. Allison decided to drop him off at his house before going to see Adam. Once she dropped Michael off, she drove to the studio where Adam was waiting for her.

Allison went to Adam's place prepared to shoot the new video. Adam welcomed Allison into the studio and gave her some new clothing to wear. She put on the clothing and came out of the dressing area. He told Allison to relax, but she was having difficulty being able to relax since she was a bit nervous. He handed her a drink of water and asked her to take a sip. She took a sip of water and then another and another until the water was gone. He put his arm around her and asked if she felt a little better. Allison said she is starting to relax. He started asking her to look at the camera, and she began to dance for him and then you can see her really letting go. Allison was dancing to the music, and Adam asked her to take off the first piece of clothing and then another and another until Allison had on a very sheer set of panties and bra. She posed as asked, and then Adam told her to take off her bra. She removed the bra, then her panties without even being asked. Adam and a photographer filmed the entire nude dancing act. Adam asked her if she is all right, and Allison could barely speak and was having a hard time standing up straight. Adam told her he was bringing in Robin to help her make this video perfect and said she will have thousands of people watching this.

Robin, a brown-haired, brown-eyed twenty-one-year old, and very familiar with these types of video, started kissing on Allison and touching her. She then removed her clothes very seductively until she too is nude. Robin took Allison and posed her into various sex positions while Adam and the photographer were shooting the entire time. After forty-five minutes, the shoot was over, and Robin got dressed and got Allison dressed before leaving. Adam checked the video as he edited it to download on the Internet.

Another hour passed, and Allison was late coming home already. Her phone had numerous missed calls from her mom and dad. Adam finally got her awake enough to drive and told her the video was terrific. She had no memory of the entire shoot. Allison said she did not feel well and got ready to leave. She kept batting her eyes trying to focus on everything. Adam gave her coffee and sent her on her way. Allison arrived home more than one and a half hours late.

When Allison went in the door at her house, her parents were frantic about where she had been. From the time she left the shoot, she had straightened up quite a bit and told her mom and dad she is sorry she is late. The parents wanted to know where she had been. Allison said she was going to work and was not feeling well, so she stopped off at Crystal's house, one of Allison's friends. They asked Allison why she didn't call and let them know so they wouldn't worry. Allison said that when she got there, she felt sick and threw up a few times before just dosing off to sleep. Paul told Jennifer to call Crystal's parents to see what they know about this, but Allison barked out, "What is this crap? What happened to 'we believe in you' and 'we trust you'?"

Paul said, "You're right, but we were worried sick. We thought something had happened to you. We called Chuck, who said you weren't there either. Why did you not let us know you did not have to work? You told us this morning you were working tonight."

"I was sick, so I did not go in. I'm sorry, can you grill me over this in the morning?" Allison went upstairs to go to bed.

When Allison went upstairs, she panicked since she had no memory of what went on at the shoot. Allison knew she was drugged but was more worried about what she did and to whom. She went online and wrote to Adam, asking him what the hell happened at the shoot and what did he give her? She then told him she wanted nothing else to do with making these videos if this is the way it's going to be. Allison was not only exhausted; she was sore all over. Allison took a shower and then checked her computer for a reply from Adam. Allison waited a few minutes but couldn't stay awake any longer, so she fell asleep.

When Allison woke up on Wednesday morning, she had a horrible headache. She got out of bed and checked her computer for a reply from Adam. Allison read the reply from Adam and then checked out the video link he sent her. She opened the website and started looking at her video. She couldn't believe what she was seeing. She was so embarrassed, and then she saw another woman she does not even know, doing things with her and to her. Allison was so sorry she made this video and wished she could stop it from being seen by anyone. She then noticed that the number of people who viewed the video was already three hundred sixty eight. She started doing the math of how much she will make even at this point and started to feel a little better. She answered the texts she received from Adam. She asked him if they can meet as soon as possible. Allison finally got dressed and was ready for school.

Allison went downstairs and saw her family. Allison's mom and dad asked how she was feeling. She stated she was feeling much better than last night. Her dad asked her again where she was last night. Allison stuck to the same story she told them the night before. She reiterated she went to her friend Crystal's house and got sick while there and then fell asleep. When she awoke from the sleep, she saw she had missed several calls from her parents. She jumped in her car and immediately drove home. Allison's parents were less than pleased with their daughter's story and the way she handled herself last night. Allison once again reminded her parents they were the ones who stated they believed her, and more importantly, they trusted her. Allison said, "I didn't do anything wrong for you to be worried about."

Allison's dad stated, "Someday, when you have children of your own, you'll understand why we were worried, and we had every right to be."

Allison apologized and asked if she could leave for school before it gets too late. The parents agreed, and Allison's mom stated she would drop Lisa off at school. Her dad told her to drive straight home tonight. Allison agreed.

When Allison got to school, her friends were waiting for her, but none of them knew her like Heather did. This was one time when she needed a best friend to lean on. Allison was confused about what happened last night and about her feelings about what happened. She was left with nowhere to turn and without a true friend in sight. Allison saw Heather, and even though they had their huge blowup, she had to confide in someone. Allison actually walked away from her posse and straight to Heather. She asked if she and Heather could talk. To Allison's surprise, Heather agreed to talk with her.

Heather asked Allison what happened to make her stoop so low as to come speak with her. Allison started crying, and for once in her life, Heather knew Allison was being sincere. Allison told Heather she had no clue what happened. When she got to the photo shoot and put on the clothes Adam gave her she then drank some water. The next thing she remembered was waking up after the shoot feeling like she had been run over by a train. Heather told Allison it is obvious Adam drugged her. Heather asked Allison if she remembered what she did on the shoot. Allison stated she did not remember any of it, but she told Heather she looked at the video, and she was horrified with what she saw.

Heather admitted she had looked at the video too since she had the password. She admitted she was so embarrassed for Allison. Allison asked Heather what she should do. Heather told her she needed to go to the police for help. Heather asked Allison didn't her dad know Detective Jack Williams. Allison told her that Jack had been to the restaurant where she works, and she knew him also. She stated she had gotten a card from Jack. Heather suggested Allison call him and turn in this jerk, Adam. Allison then told Heather about the number of hits this video had and the money she would make. Heather looked right at Allison and said, "Do you have no morals at all? These people raped you. You have to turn these jerks in."

Allison thanked Heather for listening, and she hugged her like two sisters hugging one another. Allison apologized for the way she had treated her, and they headed off to class.

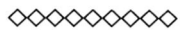

When school was done that day, Allison and Heather met in the parking lot near Allison's car. Heather told Allison she had been thinking about the situation. She asked Allison what if she told Adam that she was going to report him to the police unless he took down the website. Allison told Heather one part of her would like to do that while another part of her wanted to wait and hope the website would be a huge money maker for Adam. Allison said she was thinking then that Adam would be much easier to manipulate since taking down the website would cost him a lot more money.

Heather asked her in the meantime what if someone who becomes a member recognizes her. Allison told her that she had already met someone from the website who came into the restaurant.

Heather said, "Oh my God. What did they say to you?"

Allison stated the man told her he really liked the photos and the video.

Heather asked what else he said. Allison went on to say he asked her that if she wanted to post something bolder than the bathing suit and underwear video online, he had some suggestions. She said little did she know now the man was going to see everything. Heather asked what if he comes back to the restaurant. Allison answered, "I'm sure he'll be back now that the other video is online."

Heather asked how Allison was going to handle that. Allison just looked at Heather and said, "Nothing I can do now but deal with it."

Heather asked what she meant by that. Allison said, "As long as he just comes to the restaurant, I'll be fine. If it goes further than that, I can always call Detective Williams."

"My God, Allison, are you crazy? You have to do something now, today."

Allison said, she is going home to think about things, and she'd make a decision in the next few days.

"Please do something that is going to bring these sleazebags down."

Allison said she knows she has to do something, and she will when she decides what that thing is.

Heather and Allison got in their cars after a long hug and drove off.

When Allison got home, her mom was there. Allison asked her mom where Lisa was. Her mom told her she had dropped Lisa off at one of her friend's houses. Jennifer told Allison to come sit by her on the sofa. Allison sat down and took a deep breath.

Jennifer asked, "What's going on with you?"

Allison said, "Mom, I've just got a lot on my mind."

Her mom told Allison that sometimes life can be confusing, and it's hard to find your way. Jennifer told Allison a story of how her life was spiraling out of control when she was younger. She admitted to doing things that were not examples of a Christian lifestyle. She also admitted if Paul knew some of the things she had done in her past, they might not have even gotten married. She told Allison that her mom used to look into her eyes and tell her "I can see the devil in you."

Jennifer looked at Allison and said, "I have to say, Allison, I see that same look I had in your eyes."

Allison started to cry and told her mom she couldn't tell her everything right now, but she would when she was ready.

Her mother looked at Allison and said, "Anything you share with me I promise you I won't judge you. I will love you no matter what you are doing or what you have done."

Allison thanked her mom for telling her that story and promised to sit her mom down and tell her the whole story one day soon. The two of them looked into one another's eyes with a newfound respect for what each of them had been through. Allison was very surprised her mom shared that story, and she could not imagine her mom doing anything her dad would not have approved of. Allison got up from the sofa and went upstairs.

Allison went in to her room and sat down at her computer. She signed into her social media and started texting and talking to Adam. She was still not very comfortable with the whole website thing. She asked Adam what if she changed her mind. He responded by telling Allison she was just nervous, and everyone goes through that. He told her when she started getting her part of the money, she could buy anything she wanted and she'd feel better. She told Adam she wasn't sure if the money even mattered anymore. She stated she did not trust Adam after he gave her some type of drug to get her to do those things. She said she would have never done anything like that had it not been for the drugs.

Adam claimed he did not know what she was talking about, and if anyone gave her drugs, it must have been someone from her school. Allison said the only other person she had been near that day was her ex-boyfriend, whom she had given a ride home just before she met with Adam. Adam tried to place the blame on Michael and told Allison since he was her ex why would she have given him a ride home. Adam also said why he would have asked her for a ride if she and he were not getting along. Allison started thinking back but could not think how Michael would have gotten drugs into her system. Then she remembered Adam giving her water when he said she was stressing over the photo and video shoot. Allison remembered sipping the water he had given her three times and shortly after that not being able to recall anything.

Adam shouted at her saying that after all he was trying to do for her, now she is accusing him of drugging her to get her to do the video. Adam said he could get thousands of women to take their clothes off, and if she felt like that, he would take the site down and cancel everything. Allison said she could always go to the police, and Adam got very quiet and then said very clearly, "Allison, don't threaten me. People who make threats go missing."

Allison got very scared and told Adam she did not mean it. She told him she was sorry; she was just stressing over her parents or her family finding out. Adam told Allison, "I promised I'd protect you, and none of your family will ever know unless you make stupid choices. Stupid people get dead. Allison, don't get stupid, or you might get dead too." He told Allison the website was going fine, and they had made lots of money already. He told Allison they needed to meet so he could give her the money she'd made so far.

Allison asked if he could come to the restaurant, and Adam said, "I've got a better idea. Why don't you come here?" She told Adam she was at home and her mom would ask a lot of questions if she went out again now. Adam told Allison to come by the studio tomorrow after school. She wrote back to say she had to work tomorrow. Adam asked, "Do you want your money or not?" Allison told him she would come by there on her way to work or before she went home after work, and Adam agreed.

After Allison had stopped talking to Adam, she was replaying their conversation, and the one thing she heard that made her uneasy was the part about her being stupid and *dead*. Allison started watching television trying to take her mind off what Adam had said to her. She wanted to at least get the money he owed her, but now she was afraid to meet him anywhere. She started talking to Heather online and told her what Adam had said. Allison told Heather, "I still have not gotten the best thing to do worked out in my mind, but I will do something." Allison told Heather she was going to get off line now so she could think about what she wants to do. Heather responded with, "Either way, just know I am behind you, and if you need my help, I'm here." Allison signed out at that point. Allison went down for dinner and then right back upstairs for contemplation about her decision. She sat on her bed and wondered what it would be like to have a lot of money that belonged to her. Allison's doubt also crept in, reminding her that Adam was a thug and probably couldn't be trusted either way. Allison tried to imagine how she could get the money without meeting Adam, but she had no clue how to make it happen.

During the night, while Allison and her family slept, a man on the website was viewing the video and the pictures. This man sat at his computer mesmerized by the video, and he made a realization during the video. This man had seen this young lady before, and he kept watching the video over and over. The man would stop the video and play certain sections repeatedly, looking at her facial expressions and thinking back to when he saw her last. The man signed into the "More Information" app to get the region of the country this young lady was located in. He now knew where she was, and now his quest was to pinpoint the exact location. The man sat by the computer for most of the night playing this same video and imagining it was him in the video having fun with this young gorgeous girl. He loved the young girl playing and dancing for the camera. It was as if the young girl was looking straight at the man and teasing him with her moves and eyes. The man vows to follow this girl's video until he finds her for himself.

On Thursday morning, September 19, Allison was awakened by an incoming text on her telephone. Allison got out of the bed to see who the text was from and what the text was about. The text was from Adam reminding her to stop by the studio today or this evening. She replied she would be by sometime today or this evening if she gets off work on time. Adam texted back, Allison needs to make time. She told Adam she had to go take a shower and get ready for school. Allison got off the phone and started getting ready. When she was done, she grabbed her books and ran down for breakfast.

Once Allison got downstairs to quickly eat something, everyone asked her how she was doing. She replied she is doing fine and hopes all of them are. Allison hugged her mom and dad, grabbed Lisa, and took off out the door. Allison dropped Lisa at school and drove to her school parking lot. Once at the lot, Heather was waiting for her friend, and the two girls smiled just seeing one another.

Heather and Allison started chatting immediately and seemed to have never had any issues in the past at all. The two girls bonded together and seemed to be as good friends as any two people could be. Heather and Allison spoke very quietly so no one else could hear their conversation. Heather told Allison she could hardly even sleep last night. Allison said she too had a restless night. Then Allison told Heather she is supposed to meet Adam later today or this evening. Heather told her friend to please not meet with this guy. Heather said she is so afraid for Allison's well-being. Allison told Heather she is considering not going to the meeting to see what Adam will do next but is afraid what he might do if she doesn't show. Heather advised Allison to call the police and get Detective Williams to sit down with her, and for Allison to explain this mess to him. Allison said she doesn't think she is ready for that yet, but she might reconsider if necessary. Heather said to Allison, "These people are criminals, and they need to be handled by people who are skilled for this. Call the police."

Allison said, "Thank you again for your concern," and the two girls headed off to math class.

When class was over and school dismissed, Allison came to her car only to find a note on her windshield. Allison took the note out from under her windshield wiper, and when she read the note, she immediately jumped into her car and sped away.

Allison arrived at the restaurant to work until closing at 9:00 p.m. When she walked into the restaurant, the same two new customers she had told Adam about before were there again. Allison asked one of the new customers how they heard about the restaurant. The customer replied they had heard good things about the waitress at this place. Allison immediately became suspicious and embarrassed at the same time. She couldn't help but wonder if these people are looking at her fully clothed or if they are seeing her like she was in the video. Allison asked the customer who it was that recommended the restaurant and the waitress. The customers just shrugged their shoulders.

Allison caught them staring at her several times, especially when she was leaning over cleaning tables. Finally, Allison couldn't stand not knowing anymore, so she went over to the two men and just flat out asked them if the reason they were there was regarding her posting some photos online. The two men sort of chuckled and asked her where they could see these photos. Allison just rolled hers eyes and said, "All men are perverts and Peeping Toms." The two men told Allison they would gladly pay to see them if she'd give them the address. What Allison didn't know was during the time she was asking the men about the photos, John, the busboy, had been listening the entire time.

When Allison got her break, she was standing at the end of the counter, sipping her soda when John walked up to her and told her he overheard her talking to the men. John went on to say he would love to see the photos too. Allison told John he could drop dead for all she cared. John told Allison he was going to look at websites to see if he could find the right one with her on it. She just looked at him and just shook her head in disbelief. She couldn't imagine her day being any worse. Allison knew this whole video and photo website deal was going to blow up in her face, and all she wanted at this point was out. Allison called her mom and told her she was ready to sit down with her when she got home from work and tell her everything.

When Allison's shift was over, and she was getting ready to leave, she knew she was not going over to Adam's like she had told him she would. Allison left the restaurant bound for home. After a couple of minutes, Allison noticed a car following her. She just knew it had to be Adam, so she tried to get home as quickly as she could. The road Allison travelled was dark with very few homes along the way. The trip going home usually took Allison twenty minutes or so. Allison reached for her purse and grabbed her phone, and just as she was about to dial her mom and dad, the car behind her rammed into the back of her car causing her to drop her telephone. Allison's car swerved all over the road. Allison panicked after the car hit the rear of her vehicle again, causing her to almost lose control of her car. The car following her finally pulled alongside her, and she could not make out the identity of the person in it. All at once, the person veered to the right, and the driver ran Allison off the road.

Allison's mom and dad began to worry where Allison was when she didn't come home from work. When Allison was not at home by 10:30 p.m. they began calling her cell phone but got no answer. Paul and Jennifer both left messages for Allison to call them right away as they were both very worried. Jennifer began to call Allison's friends including Heather and several others, but no one had seen her. When Jennifer called Heather, she was frantic since it was now well after 11:30 p.m. Heather was worried as well, and she told Jennifer to please let her know if she heard from Allison. Paul told Jennifer to stay there in case Allison called or came home as he was going to look for her. Neither parent called the police right away since Allison had just been pretty late coming home recently. Paul had traced Allison's route home and saw no signs of Allison or her vehicle. Paul called Jennifer to see if she had heard from Allison, but Jennifer told him she had not. Paul told Jennifer to call the police, and he'd be home soon.

Shortly after Paul got back home about midnight on Thursday, the police arrived at their door. The policemen came into the house as Paul and Jennifer told the police their daughter was missing. Jennifer had also called Landon and told him Allison was missing. The police asked the parents when was the last time they had contact with their daughter. Jennifer responded by saying her daughter had called while at work tonight but just to say she wanted to sit down and talk with her when she arrived at home. The policemen told the parents they were very sorry, but Allison would not officially be missing until she had been gone for twenty-four hours without any contact.

Paul was very unhappy with this answer, and he told the police she had never been out all night. Paul and Jennifer told the police their daughter is only sixteen years old. Lisa, the thirteen year old, was begging the police to go look for her sister. The policemen asked if anyone had traced Allison's route to see if she stopped off somewhere. Paul stated he had gone from their house all the way to the restaurant and back but saw no signs of their daughter. About this time, Landon, Allison's older brother, arrived at his parent's home. The police asked if they had called all of Allison's friends, and Jennifer said she had already done that too. Jennifer told the police their daughter was at Crystal's house when she was late coming home before, but she did not know the phone number or last name for this friend.

The policemen stated once again there was nothing they could do until Allison had been gone for twenty-four hours. Jennifer was crying uncontrollably and begging the police, but there was nothing they could do. The police got a description of Allison's car and the license plate number. The police said they would keep an eye out for the car, but that's all they could do. They told the parents to call them tomorrow evening after 8:00 p.m. if they had not heard from Allison by then. The police told the parents she's probably at one of her friend's houses and just fell asleep. The police were sure Allison was fine. Landon told the police, "Are you kidding me? You're not going to even look for her? This is my sixteen-year-old sister. I can't believe what I'm hearing." The police left the home.

Landon and Paul decided they were going to look for Allison if it took all night. About 3:00 a.m. Friday, both Paul and Landon were exhausted from looking all over town, so they returned home where they could pray together. Paul, Jennifer, Landon, and Lisa prayed the remainder of the night for Allison's safe return, but there was no sign of Allison. After daylight, the family still prayed for Allison's return, but reality was starting to settle in. Paul decided he was going to call Detective Williams and see if he could do something to find Allison.

On Friday morning about 7:00 a.m., detective Williams came to Paul's and Jennifer's home. Detective Jack felt very deeply for the predicament the family was in, but he told the family that by law, Allison's case would not get anywhere until the twenty-four hours were up. Jack told the family not to go into Allison's room for any reason so if they had to do an investigation, the forensic team would see the room undisturbed. Jack said he would go to the school and see if he could speak to any of Allison's friends. He wanted to give the family some kind of hope and felt he would have to interview all of Allison's friends anyway. He told the family he couldn't promise anything, but he would ask around.

Paul remembered Allison telling him about the incident regarding Chuck and John at the restaurant, so he told Landon what happened. Landon told his dad, "Let's go to the restaurant and talk to these guys." Paul and Landon headed out to the restaurant later Friday morning to see if either one of the men knew anything that might help them find Allison. When Paul and Landon arrived at the restaurant, they went inside, and Paul asked Chuck if everything was all right last night and informed them that Allison never came home.

Chuck told the men everything seemed to be fine when Allison left. There were no problems during her shift that he noticed anyway. Chuck then called John over to ask him if he knew of any problems last night. John asked was there some problem with the princess? Landon grabbed John by the throat and shoved him against the wall then told him that Allison did not make it home.

John told Landon to turn him loose that he did not know what happened after Allison left. Landon told John he knew he had been hassling Allison, and he better hope he didn't have anything to do with her disappearance. John said he had not seen Allison after she left, and Allison made accusations against him and Chuck, but she had lied.

Landon looked directly at John and said, "You better hope I don't find out you ever laid a hand on my sister, or I'll kill you."

Paul put his hand on Landon's shoulder and told him to come along since this is not helping them find Allison. Paul told Chuck and John he had already spoken to the police regarding Allison's disappearance, and John spoke right up and said, "The police aren't going to do anything until she's missing twenty-four hours. Even I know that." Paul asked John how he would know that. John said, "I had a friend go missing one time, and the police did nothing. The police are more interested in putting people who are innocent in jail." John turned and walked away. Both Landon and Paul looked at one another trying to figure out what that statement meant or had to do with anything. Paul and Landon exited the building and drove back home.

When Paul and his son got back home, there had been no change in the situation. Jennifer stated there had been no phone calls from Allison or the police on her whereabouts. Lisa had become so upset over the situation she had become physically ill. Jennifer had to call their family doctor to get him to come over to administer to Lisa. When the family doctor arrived, he treated Lisa and gave her some medication to help her relax. The doctor told the family he hoped Allison would be found alive and well. The doctor also told the family Lisa would sleep for a while as she needed some rest. Jennifer asked how the visit went at the restaurant. Paul told her they really didn't get any useful information as to Allison's location. Landon told his mom about the whole situation with John and how he had nothing good to say about Allison. Paul spoke up and asked Landon if he understood the comment John made regarding that missing person thing. Landon told him he had no idea, but he did find it odd John would know so much about missing person practices. Paul agreed.

The family spent the rest of the day calling everyone they knew, as well as launching a neighborhood search party. Paul and his family had always been there for their community and their neighbors, so now it was the neighbors' turn to help. Paul and Jennifer told the neighbors about their daughter not coming home last night and that the police couldn't do anything until Allison had been missing for twenty-four hours. Paul and Jennifer begged the neighborhood to pray for their family and Allison would be found safe. The neighbors started making posters with Allison's photo on them and then posting them on every telephone pole they could find, as well as posting them in local businesses. The neighbors were more than willing to do whatever they could to help locate Allison.

Heather called Jennifer and asked if there had been any word on Allison's location. Jennifer said they had not heard anything and were waiting for the police to get involved tonight. Jennifer asked Heather who this Crystal girl was whom Allison stayed with when she had become sick and had fallen asleep. Heather told Jennifer she was not sure but it might be someone in one of Allison's classes, but she didn't know her personally. Jennifer thought it was odd that Heather wouldn't have known this girl Crystal.

Heather asked Jennifer to please keep her posted and asked if there was anything she could do. Jennifer just asked Heather to please see if she could find this Crystal girl and if this was the one who loaned Allison those expensive diamond earrings. Heather told her the earrings were a present from her grandmother, and she did loan them to Allison. Heather got off the phone with a feeling that Adam had done something with Allison. Heather felt bad she had not been able to get Allison to call the police. She knew she should be calling the police, but she didn't want to call yet only to have Allison show up and then hate her for meddling.

Later that day, no one had any word on where Allison was, and the family was starting to lose all faith that she would be found alive. Paul and his family would never give up hope but were aware the more time had passed with no word from or about Allison was not very promising. Paul was praying as hard as he could and was asking God why this happened to his daughter.

Paul, Jennifer, Landon, and Lisa were sitting together Friday evening when Detective Jack came to their door. Jack rang the doorbell, and Paul answered the door. Paul was quite frankly expecting the news to be bad but was hoping for a miracle. Jack was welcomed into the couple's home. Jack told the family he had not really found out anything. Jack stated he had been to Allison's school, but her friends were not very helpful or forthcoming with information. Jack told the family he of course was still hoping for the best, but the family needs to be prepared for the worst, just in case. Jack advised the family the entire law enforcement department was being thrown behind this investigation. Jack wanted them to know he would not rest until he found Allison and/or the answers. Jack prayed with them before leaving.

The family sat quietly after Jack left, still praying for Allison's safe return. Every family member was also thinking about who would have done such a thing if Allison was found dead. None of the family wanted to vocalize their thoughts and possible suspicions since they had not gotten any word to confirm Allison's death. All anyone could think of was where could Allison be and what she must have been thinking if someone took her. Each family member was also thinking of all the bad things they had said over the years or arguments they had with Allison and how they all would love to see her once again.

Paul was thinking how scared Allison must have been if someone kidnapped her. He was thinking too if she was kidnapped then why have they not gotten a ransom call. Jennifer couldn't help but think about the conversation she and her daughter had regarding Allison's mind-set. Then when Allison called her mom from work last night telling her she wanted to sit down with her and tell her everything. Everything, what could be included in everything? Could Allison have been in trouble? Could Allison have been pregnant? Could someone have been abusing her? Jennifer kept thinking, *I'm her mother, I should have noticed something was wrong before now.*

Landon sat, thinking he should have been there for Allison more. He assumed if she was in trouble, she would have confided in him. He couldn't help but think he was too busy to see if she was in pain emotionally. Lisa was thinking where her sister is and whom she knew who might have hurt her sister. All Lisa could think of was Michael, who used to be her boyfriend, and then John who talked down to Allison. Each family member had their own demons in their heads and their doubts. The family sat literally in a huddle, holding one another and sobbing while they beat themselves up over their own relationship, or lack thereof, with Allison.

After a long restless and agonizing night, the family was awakened by Detective Jack ringing their doorbell on Saturday morning. Jack told the family there was no news regarding Allison, but he was here with the forensic team to go through Allison's room. Jack told the family they are going to do everything possible to find Allison hopefully alive, but if not, he is going to find out who would do such a thing and bring them before the court, and hopefully, they will be found guilty.

Jack was still talking to the family when one of the team members came downstairs and told Jack he needed to see something. Jack went upstairs, and the team had found a note on Allison's desk that read, "You can't afford not to meet me." The team took Allison's computer and other items they had confiscated back to the crime lab. The team was hoping to find clues on her computer and in her e-mail and social media accounts. Jack came back downstairs, and the family asked him what the team found upstairs. Jack said he can't talk about it yet since everything they find has to be verified before he can discuss any part of the case. He told the family they were taking Allison's computer and some of her other personal belongings and advised the parents they were also going to her school on Monday and taking everything in her locker. Jack advised the family that no stone would be unturned on this investigation, and everyone Allison knew will be interviewed. Jack couldn't help but think about the busboy at the restaurant as a potential suspect as well as whomever wrote the note they found. He also wondered what Allison had done for someone to have written such a note. He kept thinking through scenarios Allison could have been involved in that brought someone to this end. Jack was hopeful Allison would be found alive. With no ransom note or phone call, he felt the best they could hope for at this point was to find the killer or killers and Allison's body. While the forensic team picked apart Allison's life, Jack went back to look through the mug books to see if he could find anything more on the busboy, John.

On Sunday, when the family usually had their breakfast, the household was obviously not the same. Jennifer asked Paul if he was even up to having the service. Paul told Jennifer it was his duty to keep the congregation united even through his family's tough times. For the first time in years, the family did not cook together as no one wanted to cook a family meal without Allison. Landon set the table as usual with the Sunday dishes and linen napkins but left one plate off the table to recognize his sister being absent. When Jennifer saw the gesture by her son, she ran upstairs weeping. The family members were on their own to eat something if they felt like it. Like many Sundays before, the family left the house together for the church.

When the family arrived at church, they could not believe their eyes at what they saw. There were so many people at the church there was literally no place to park. Paul had huge tears in his eyes to see how many people showed up to support his family and what they were going through.

Paul stopped their vehicle on the lawn of the church, and the family got out. Hundreds of people came and hugged each Tuttle family member individually and escorted them one by one into the church.

The church was packed from one end to the other there was standing room only. As Paul began the service with a prayer, he was so moved he broke down and could not finish the prayer, so one of the deacons finished it for him. The remainder of the service was held by the congregation members each telling a story of how the pastor and/or one of the family members had helped them in some way or had been there for them in a tough situation. The service ended with singing by the whole congregation, and each participant coming by and telling the family they were there in this time of need.

Paul and his family were escorted out just like when they came in, and the final participant in today's service was Detective Jack Williams. Jack hugged each Tuttle family member and told them he was praying for Allison's safe return.

On Monday, Jack went back to the school where the girls were not very helpful. Jack knew they all knew something but for some reason were hiding that from him. When

Jack started the investigation, he began by interviewing the teachers. He asked them into the office the school had set aside for him. For the most part, the teachers all stated Allison was a good student and shared their stories with him regarding Allison's personality.

When it came time for Jack to interview Allison's math teacher, she had a much different story to tell the investigator. The teacher told Jack that Allison was very distant from time to time and over the last few weeks Allison had shown up in school with expensive jewelry on and more makeup than she had been wearing. The teacher also noticed Allison was very offensive to some of her peers if they weren't in her click. Jack asked the teacher if she had told any of this to Allison's parents. The teacher said she probably should have, but she had not. Jack asked had she reported any of this to the school counselor, and once again, the teacher said she had not. He asked if Allison's attendance record was good, and the teacher answered yes except for one day recently, when Allison was asked to take a pop quiz—Allison stated she was not feeling well and wanted to go to the nurse's office. The teacher stated she knew it was only because Allison was not prepared for the test, but she allowed her to go to the office anyway. She gave Allison a hall pass to go see the nurse. Allison never came back into the class, so the teacher assumed she was with the nurse.

Jack asked why the teacher did not check on Allison once she did not return to class. The teacher stated she just assumed by the time the nurse let her go back to class the class would have been dismissed. Jack asked the teacher what happened next, and the teacher said by the time Allison came to class the next morning, she had gotten a note from the nurse stating Allison never got to her office. The teacher then said she asked Allison why she never went to the nurse's office, and Allison claimed the nurse was out, so she went home to lie down. Jack told the teacher he would check out this story and get back to her.

Jack finished his interviews with the teachers by speaking with the principal of the school and the guidance counselor. Then Jack left to speak to Jennifer.

Jack arrived at Allison's home later that Monday and rang the doorbell. Paul answered the door with an anxious look on his face when he saw Detective Jack Williams. Jack told Paul there was no news on Allison, but he needed to speak to Jennifer. Paul welcomed Jack inside and went to get Jennifer who was upstairs with Lisa. Jennifer came downstairs, and they went into another room. Jack told Landon and Lisa he needed to speak to the others in private. Jack closed the door to the room, and they all sat down. Jack asked Jennifer about the day Allison left school after telling her math teacher she was not feeling well. Jack asked if they did know where Allison went. Jennifer and Paul told Jack that Allison had told them she went to a home of a friend of hers, Crystal. Jack asked if she knew Crystal's last name, and Jennifer told him no. He asked if anyone else might know the girl's last name or where she lives, and Jennifer told him she had spoken to Heather about this Crystal girl. Jack asked if she knew the address of Heather, and Jennifer gave it to him with the phone number.

Jennifer asked if Jack thought either one of the girls had anything to do with their daughter being missing. Jack just said he needed to speak to them immediately, especially Crystal. Paul asked why was it so important to speak to Crystal, and Jack responded that according to Allison's class schedule, she did not go to class with a girl named Crystal. The parents were shocked, and then Jennifer said Heather was supposed to get back to her with the name and phone number of Crystal. Jennifer then said Heather knew there was no Crystal when she spoke to her. Why would Heather lie? Jennifer told Jack when she had spoken to Heather regarding the diamond earrings he had mentioned to her that Heather told her they were given to her by her grandmother, and she loaned them to Allison to wear. Jack asked the parents to keep this information to themselves, that he shouldn't have even shared this with them.

Paul asked if Jack thought Allison was still alive. Jack told the parents to remain positive since no body had been found, Allison may very well still be alive. Jack prayed with the parents again and then left so he could follow up on these leads. Paul and Jennifer went over and hugged their children. Landon asked if it was bad news, and Paul replied it was information but not bad news. "Keep the faith. Allison is depending on us for that."

Detective Jack went over to Heather's house after she had gotten out of school. Jack went to the door and introduced himself to the mother then asked if Heather was at home. Her mom wanted to know what a detective wanted with her daughter. Jack just explained he had a few questions for her regarding the disappearance of Allison. Heather's mom told Jack she was sorry to hear about Allison being missing, and it also scared her to death with Heather going back and forth to school alone. Jack assured her the department was doing all they could to find her. Heather's mom asked Jack in and then went to get Heather.

When Heather came down the stairs, Jack noticed she looked like she had seen a ghost. Jack introduced himself to her and then started asking her questions. Jack asked Heather if she knew the last name of Crystal whom Allison stayed with several days ago. Heather stated she was not sure she knew Crystal. Detective Jack told Heather that Allison's mom just told him that she had spoken to her regarding Crystal and you confirmed you knew her but was unsure of her address or last name. You even told Allison's mom you'd get the information and call her with it.

Heather just said she thought Allison's mom misunderstood. What Heather meant was the girl was in one of Allison's classes but not one where she and Heather were in together. Jack said, "Really, what class?" Heather told Jack she wasn't sure. Jack asked Heather to describe Crystal. Heather started, "Ahhhh, she is sixteen and like about five feet or so with ahhhh blondish hair and sort of average."

Jack looked right into Heather's eyes and told her she was lying. Heather's mom told Jack to stop right there. "You can't come into my house and tell my daughter she is a liar. I'm getting my daughter an attorney." Then Heather's mom told Jack he better leave.

Jack was astonished at the way Heather and her mom handled this interview. He thought an innocent person wouldn't need an attorney. He couldn't help but wonder what Heather was hiding. He was starting to wonder what's going on in this small town. One girl was missing, and her best friend was lying about her involvement.

It was late in the day, and school had been dismissed, so Jack would have to start fresh in the morning interviewing the students. Jack was thinking Allison has now been missing for more than ninety-six hours with no real clues to follow.

About 3:00 a.m., Tuesday morning, September 24, there was a knock on Detective Jack's door, and as he went to the door, he could see it was an officer. Jack opened the door, and the officer told Jack they found a young girl dead. Jack asked if it was Allison, and the officer stated they thought they had better come get him first. Jack asked where the body was found, and the officer answered the body was found at a nearby convenience store, and it was found by a garbage man picking up a dumpster. The garbage man stated he saw something in the dumpster before he dumped it into the truck. He got out and looked at it and that's when he saw the body. The officer stated they had called the medical examiner and the coroner, but they had not arrived yet. Jack got dressed, and they headed to the crime scene.

By the time they got to the crime scene, the coroner and the medical examiner were there. Jack asked the medical examiner what he could tell about the body. Of course, the news media was there asking if this was the body of Allison Tuttle, and they were told the police were still investigating and would not release the identity of the victim until the family of the victim was notified. Jack asked the medical examiner again what he could tell about the body. The medical examiner showed Jack the body with the tape over her mouth and her hands bound by duct tape behind her back.

Jack said, "Oh my God."

The medical examiner stated this is the body of a young girl, approximately fifteen to eighteen years of age, with blonde hair, blue eyes, and slim build. The medical examiner stated he believed this to be the body of Allison Tuttle based on the photos he had to go by. The medical examiner said he would know more after the autopsy. He stated the dental records would be the key. Then Jack asked if she had been violated, and the medical examiner told him she had been. But since the girl had been missing for more than three days, all he could say was she had been sexually active just before her death.

The medical examiner stated he would know more after he checked her for vaginal bruising. He added her cause of death was believed to be erotic asphyxiation. Jack could not believe this was happening to a local girl whom he knew. Jack and the forensic team stayed and examined the crime scene thoroughly after the medical examiner and the coroner had left with the body. Jack told the medical examiner to call him when he knew the identity for sure. Jack and the team found other clues in the dumpster. The team found what they believed to be the woman's shoes, a note in the pocket of her pants, and a piece of jewelry. The team also had the tape from the woman's hands to be examined as well as the tape on her mouth. The team would also have any skin or other source for DNA from under her nails.

After several hours had passed, the medical examiner called Jack, and he took a deep breath as he knew this was going to be her body. The medical examiner confirmed it was in fact Allison. The medical examiner then told Jack one other thing he was not prepared for: Allison was approximately four weeks pregnant. He asked the M.E. when the full DNA panel would be completed and the M.E. said the full panel of testing including the fetus usually takes four weeks but if he rushed it closer to three weeks. Jack could not believe what he just heard regarding the pregnancy and had no idea how this family was going to take this information.

About 8:00 a.m., Tuesday, Jack arrived at Paul and Jennifer's home and rang the doorbell. Paul answered the door and just the look on Jack's face told him his daughter had been found dead. Jack stepped inside the house and told the family Allison's body was found about 2:00 a.m. in a dumpster at a convenience store. They broke down in tears. And then Paul asked how she died. Jack told them she had died

from asphyxiation. Paul asked what condition Allison was in when they found her, and Jack told him, "You don't want to know, it wasn't pretty."

Jack asked Paul if he could speak with him in private, and the two men walked away from the others for a minute. Once away from the others, Jack told Paul that Allison was four weeks pregnant.

Paul said, "That can't be true."

Jack said, "It's a positive result. The medical examiner found it during the autopsy."

Paul asked by who, and Jack stated they were still working on the testing process to find out. The two men went back to the others. Jack told the family that Allison was found in a dumpster by a garbage man. Paul asked about Allison's car, and Jack said they had not found it. Jack went on to say he was very sorry, and he would let them be alone to grieve. Paul asked when they could get their daughter, and Jack told them they have to process the DNA which could take weeks, and he would call them when the body was ready for viewing for positive ID. Once again, Jack prayed with the family before he left the house.

Jack was so frustrated with the current situation he had forgotten today was Tuesday, and he needed to follow up with the school to collect interviews from the students. Jack had just gotten started with the interviews when the ME called and asked him to come by there. Jack told the medical examiner he would be right there. He got to the medical examiner's office and went inside to see what he had found in the results. The M.E. told Jack it was going to take some time to determine who the father of the baby, was and he was having a postmortem viability test performed to get that started.

The medical examiner told Jack they had found several new clues. First of all, based on the angle of the body when she was found and the amount of decomposition, he estimated Allison was killed approximately twenty to twenty-four hours after she had gotten off work on that Thursday night. The M.E. also said Allison was killed somewhere else and dropped in the dumpster. Second of all, there were some fibers in the adhesive from the duct tape, which turned out to be some type of fiberglass or a fiberglass derivative. Thirdly, Allison was involved in some type of sexual activity, but she did have some vaginal bruising indicating there was some rough sex or some type of forced sex. Fourth, there were also bruises on her ankles indicating she was tied or bound to something. Finally, the shoes found in the dumpster did not fit her feet. The piece of jewelry they found in the dumpster was nothing special and could be bought almost anywhere. The M.E. stated the note in her pocket was so contaminated by the liquid in the dumpster there were no fingerprints they could use. Jack asked if the M.E. had found any DNA under Allison's nails, and the M.E. said the nails had been polished, and any DNA had been wiped away.

Jack asked the M.E. if he did not have any good news. The M.E. told Jack he wished he could give him some good news, but based on what he saw, someone knew what he was doing. "This suspect has done this before and is very good at it. The suspect knew, by throwing her body into the dumpster for that period of time, there would be very little chance we could trace anything from the crime scene."

Jack asked if the convenience store had video cameras, and the M.E. stated he was not going to like the answer. Yes, they do have cameras, but they do not work, and he would bet money the suspect knew that also. Jack asked the M.E. if they had checked to see who owned the store, and the M.E. stated they had not. The M.E. did not feel like they were involved at the time. Jack said if the store was handpicked maybe now is the time to find out. Jack said that if the suspect knew all about the area, they must be from here. Jack asked the M.E. if he knew of any other crimes like this in the area at any time before now. The M.E. stated he was not aware of any.

Jack left the M.E.'s office about 1:00 p.m. that Tuesday and went to visit the convenience store owner. Jack arrived at the store and started asking questions about the murder. The owner first said he did not speak good English, and when Jack pressed him for information, did not want to get involved. Jack told the owner he could answer questions at his store or at the station. Jack asked the owner when the dumpster was usually emptied, and the owner stated once a week unless they called to ask for a pickup sooner. The store owner asked when the body was put in the dumpster. Jack told him most likely Friday night or early Saturday morning. The owner stated he was not on duty that night, but his son-in-law was and he would be here tonight about 6:00 p.m.

Jack asked for the address for the son-in-law, and the owner gave it to him. Jack asked the owner why he said he did not want to get involved. The owner then said anyone who would do this to a young girl was someone he did not need coming after him for helping the police. Jack shook his head and told the owner he understood, but Jack also asked the owner what if it had been his daughter. "Would you want someone to get involved or just sit by and do nothing?" The store owner found himself shaking his head too. Jack asked why they had not smelled the body before, and the owner said the dumpster always stunk, and they just thought it was nothing more than that. Jack thanked him for his time but warned the owner not to tell his son-in-law he was coming or he would be back.

Jack went to visit the son-in-law of the owner from the store. When Jack arrived at the man's home, there was no answer at the door. He walked around outside of the man's trailer and saw no signs of the man. Jack decided to wait until later when the man would be at work and visit him there. He left the man's trailer and headed back to the Tuttle's house.

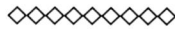

Jack arrived at the Tuttle's house about 2:00 p.m. and rang the bell. Paul came to the door and let Jack inside. Jack asked where the rest of the family was, and Paul told him they were trying to get some rest as best they could. Jack commented he was actually glad as he really wanted to speak to Paul privately. Jack started by telling Paul how sorry he was they had to go through this. Jack said he could not fathom how hard this must be. Paul asked if there had been any news on the DNA fetus test. But all Jack could say was it takes time, possibly four weeks or more and a special lab to get the records. Paul asked Jack to promise him he would not quit until this monster was found. Jack promised, and then Paul said, "Jack, I can't believe I'm saying this. When you find him, I hope he goes for a gun, and you have to shoot him dead." Jack thought how odd this was coming from a pastor. But he was a father first, and a pastor second.

Paul asked Jack how he could be of help. Jack told Paul, "These were going to be tough questions and some of the questions might be from left field but please try to understand I'm asking these questions for a certain reason. Also understand I can't go into detail on some of these, but I am looking for an answer." Jack asked if Paul had noticed anything out of the ordinary lately with Allison.

Paul asked, "What do you mean 'out of the ordinary'?"

"Any new friends or strange behavior?"

Paul cautiously said, "No more than normal, I guess."

Jack asked if Paul had heard Allison talking on the phone anytime recently, and Paul said he did not listen in on her conversations. Jack then asked if Allison had any new boyfriends or recent boyfriend splits. Paul stated the only one he knew of was a boy named Michael from her school. Jack asked if the split was worse than normal. Paul told Jack he would have to talk to Jennifer about that. Paul did say Allison had complained about her boss, Chuck, and the busboy from the restaurant being perverts and trying to feel all over her. Jack noted Paul's comments in his investigation book.

Then Jack asked the hardest question of all. Jack asked if Paul knew Allison was sexually active. Paul told Jack, "I had no idea my daughter was having sex." Jack dropped his head and Paul asked, "What are you not telling me?"

Jack said they did a toxicology panel on Allison, and they found some type of drug in her system. Paul just sat there and then asked, "Do I want to know what else they found?"

Jack responded, "I can't comment on that." Jack thanked Paul for his time and left.

Jack was called back to the office about 4:00 p.m., Tuesday, to see what the team found on Allison's computer they had taken from the Tuttle's home. He arrived back at his office and was told there were some very interesting e-mails on Allison's computer. Jack asked to see the e-mails. While the technician brought up the e-mails, Jack sat there in amazement at what he was seeing. He looked at the two videos and the photos and came to the realization no one knew this girl as much as they thought they did.

Jack noticed in the first video that Allison appeared to be acting on her own, the same as in the photos. Jack just sat there, wondering how in the world he was going to break this to her parents. As Jack watched the outrageous video, he was looking for clues as well as watching all the sex games the two women were playing. It was clear they were taking direction from someone off screen. Jack wondered what sick bastard could direct these young women to do these things to one another. One of the technicians stopped the video and focused their equipment on the younger girl. He told Jack to look at the girl's expression and her eyes. Jack responded she is stoned or on something. In the second video with Allison being drugged, she was doing things to the older girl and allowing her to do sex acts on Allison that Jack did not believe she would have allowed had she not been drugged. The technician stated clearly she had something in her system based on her pupils.

Jack asked if there was anything on any of the sex toys, such as a logo or patent mark, that would tell us where these toys were bought and/or made. The technicians said they would try to run these toys down. Jack asked the technician if there was any clue as to where this was shot. The technician told Jack it was impossible to tell from the video, and there was no trail to follow since the company that posted these videos used different ghost locations from all over the world to hide their identity. This video had bounced off servers in all parts of the country as well. This first video looks like it came from a server in the Philippines, while the second video looked like it came from a server in North Korea.

Jack asked if they could trace the e-mail another way, and the technician responded even the e-mails are bounced off servers that could be anywhere in the world too. The IP address has phantom locations, and these people can make it appear to be anywhere by using satellite connections. It's like watching a shell game where what you see is not what you think you see. The technician also said these guys are very professional, and when Allison got mixed up with them, she was way out of her league. The technician also said that according to the professionalism of the people who posted these videos, he would bet these were being seen by hundreds of thousands of people all over the world.

Jack told the technicians what he was concerned with was how in the heck this girl ever met someone like this in this small town. One of the technicians also showed Jack the only clue from this video was a slight reflection in a window of someone, but the image was not even clear enough to see if it was male or female. Jack said, "Maybe we should try to find out who this other woman was in the video and do facial recognition software." The technicians told Jack that would mean bringing in the FBI. Jack told them to hold off notifying anyone outside of their team. He asked the technicians, "What could we do with these videos to find who did this?"

The technicians responded, "All we can do is try to follow the trail as far as we can and see where that goes." They also showed Allison's e-mails from other people. There were a few from an unknown and an untraceable address that had been removed from Allison's computer. The technicians told Jack the trace was still in the computer, but the text in the e-mails was removed from the hard drive. Jack asked if they had any idea where they came from, and the technicians stated they were still working through the process. He also saw e-mails from Heather talking about some guy named Fred coming to Allison's work. There was no other reference other than that.

There was another e-mail where Heather and Allison were referring to some guys coming into the restaurant that Allison did not know at all. Allison also talked about an argument she had with some guy named Michael. Jack remembered Paul telling him Michael used to be her boyfriend. Jack also saw other e-mail from Allison's other friends even though some of the e-mails didn't sound so friendly. There was one e-mail where a girl was threatening Allison about some expensive diamond earrings, which Jack remembered seeing Allison wearing when he was at the restaurant the first time he went by there.

Jack kept wondering who the father of her baby was and why she allowed herself to get pregnant. Jack kept thinking what this girl was into so deep that it got her killed. He was beginning to wonder if Allison was secretly having sex for money. Was she selling drugs or taking drugs and that's why she met with this tragic end? Jack sat there a while with his mind racing through all that has happened. Jack's team told him to go home and try to rest; he had been working this case since 3:00 a.m., and it's now well after 7:00 p.m. Jack wanted to continue to work the case since he felt he was letting the family down by trying to rest. But the team told him, "You're no good to anyone without rest. Plus, you'll see things better after some much-needed rest." Jack finally agreed and went home to make an attempt at resting. The last thought Jack had before finally falling asleep was where is Allison's car. Why have they not found it?

When Jack woke up about 5:00 a.m. on Wednesday, he was ready to get back in the hunt. Jack went down to his office and prepared a huge dry erasable board to put down all of the clues thus far and the steps his team had taken so he would follow the investigation better. Jack was still trying to get his mind wrapped around this video ring and how they got started in this area. Jack started writing on the board with:

1. Local sixteen-year-old girl was missing.
2. Allison was pregnant.
3. Same girl found dead in dumpster outside a store.
4. Video pornography ring connected to the same girl.
5. Expensive diamond earrings.
6. DNA wiped clean from fingernails of girl.
7. Erotic asphyxiation.
8. Violated, raped, or sex.

9. Piece of jewelry found in dumpster.
10. Note in Allison's pocket.
11. Duct tape on mouth and hands behind the back.
12. Woman's shoes in dumpster.
13. Pornographer
14. Drugs
15. Michael?
16. Allison's boss, Chuck
17. Busboy
18. Various men seeing video
19. ?????
20. Photographer
21. Other female in video
22. Car missing
23. Purse missing
24. Why?
25. Cell phone missing

As Jack was writing on the board, he kept thinking none of this makes any sense. Jack sat down, thinking what he should do next. So he decided to go speak to the other kids at Allison's school. Jack got into his cruiser and went over to the school to get the interviews started. The principal set an office aside for the detective for as long as he needed. Jack began by getting a class list of students for each of

Allison's classes. One by one the students came in to see the detective and be interviewed.

When Jack got down to Allison's click of friends, he carefully interviewed them at great length. Jack asked if they had ever been present when Allison was harassed by another student. Each of the girls told Jack they had been present when Allison and Michael had several arguments, and Michael made threats against Allison. One of the girls told Jack that Michael was yelling at Allison saying, "You'll be sorry you treated me this way." Jack was taking notes of all the worthwhile comments so he could follow up on them.

Some of the girls told Jack about this guy who was standing near Allison's car one day after school and after Allison walked up to him, she certainly looked like she knew him too. After Allison drove off in her car, the man jumped into his car and sped off after her. Jack asked for a description of the car, but each girl seemed to remember something differently from the other, and none of them could even agree as to the color of the car or the make. Jack then asked for a description of the man, and all the girls could agree on was the man was cute. Some had the man standing six feet tall and others five feet tall. The other thing the girls agreed upon was the man was someone they had never seen before. Jack asked one of the girls if she knew this girl named Crystal. The girl responded she was not sure who Jack was referring to.

Jack asked the girls if they had ever witnessed Allison's boss giving her a hard time, and some of them stated Jack should check Allison's ass for fingerprints, and they were sure he'd find the fingerprints of her boss and that slime ball busboy. Jack asked the girls if they ever heard Heather and Allison argue. Each girl in their click remembered several times the two girls argued and even once when Heather told Allison she would tell everything she knew about Allison's activities. Jack asked if the girls knew what she meant. No one seemed to know exactly what that meant, but one of the girls also told Jack that Allison always had extra money and often wore expensive jewelry and nice makeup.

Jack told the girls Allison was working; maybe the money came from her tips at work. The girls told Jack maybe the extra money came from her boss at the restaurant; he seemed to have a thing for her. Jack asked one of the girls if she had seen the diamond earrings Allison had been wearing, and she stated she loaned the earrings to Allison. Jack smiled and said, "Are you sure you want to lie to the police? I have heard two different people tell me they loaned these earrings to Allison. Now, do you want me to arrest you, or do you want to tell me the truth?"

The girl stated Allison had asked all of her friends to say they loaned her the earrings if anyone asked. Jack asked when that was, and the girl told him it was right after her parents had questioned Allison about the earrings. Jack asked the girls if they knew anything about this busboy at the restaurant. Each one of the girls all thought he was some sort of criminal the way he acts and brag's about things he's done. Jack asked if they knew what kind of things. One girl told Jack she heard he had been jammed up over some girl and that was why he moved here. Jack thanked the girls for their input and their time. Jack wanted to sit down with Heather, but her mother refused to let her be interviewed.

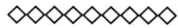

Jack started interviewing the members of the football team. Several of the football players commented on Allison's demeanor. When Jack asked what the players meant, they all agreed they did not want to speak ill of the dead. Jack told them it would really help him solve the crime if he had all of the details to what Allison was doing as well as her impact on others. Most of the players told Detective Jack that Allison had a strange personality, and from time to time, she was so moody you never knew what moment she was going to bite your head off. A couple of the players also said Allison was a flirt with anyone who had something she wanted. One by one, the players told Jack they were worried about Allison since she would use anyone to get what she wanted and not think anything in the world about it.

Jack was shocked to hear these things from Allison's peers. Some of the players remembered the confrontation between Allison and the busboy at the restaurant the night of the football game. They agreed the busboy was hot for Allison, and they squared off in the restaurant and had a heated encounter, yelling and making threats. The players also remembered Allison yelling at her boss, telling him if he didn't keep his hands off her, she would tell his wife.

On the same night, the players told Jack the boss threatened to fire Allison if she didn't work. Several of the players also stated the boss of the restaurant would have his hands all over her when he thought no one was watching. Jack told the guys he appreciated their taking the time to sit down with him, and their information was crucial to solving this case. Jack let the guys go back to what they were doing and told them if he needed to speak with them further, he would let them know. Jack went back to the office to ask the principal if Michael was in class today, and the principal checked with the teachers, who told him Michael did not attend school today. So Jack told the principal he would interview Michael tomorrow.

Jack got a call from the M.E.'s office as he was leaving the high school. The M.E. told him they were finished with Allison's body as far as DNA evidence tests were concerned but were waiting for the panel to come back, and they had found some other clues from what they processed. The M.E. told Jack the body could not be released until he was sure nothing else would be needed for the panel of tests. Jack told the M.E. he would be right there.

At five o'clock on Wednesday afternoon, Jack arrived back at the M.E.'s office to get the updated information. When Jack went into the office, he asked the M.E. what they had found. He began by telling Jack that not only did the toxicology report and the autopsy show birth control pills in Allison's system; she also had some traces of ecstasy in her system, as well as PT-141. Jack asked what the heck that is. The M.E. told Jack it was an experimental drug not released to the public as yet. He went on to say that as far as he knew, this drug was used in Europe but had not been used in the United States.

Jack asked the M.E. to tell him about it. He told Jack, "It is a nasal spray to end all nasal sprays, a new and hugely effective brain-stroking libido-licking sex-drive-boosting drug, and even if it is half as effective as some of the amazing human trials indicate, it will revolutionize sex in a way Viagra could only dream about and which Ecstasy can only wink at. It works for both men and women. It is unaffected by food or alcohol. It is nonaddictive, easy to use, has no serious physical side effects. It works by opening/stimulating against the same channels in the brain, as opposed to the bloodstream, like Viagra, that fire up when you get turned on. It is not Ecstasy, but it certainly could be the designer club drug of the new millennium."

Jack asked how this could be in Allison's system, and the M.E. stated it had to come into this country through the black market, and obviously, these people are very well-connected. Jack tells the M.E. they may be in big trouble if this drug is already here. He said this Ecstasy and PT-141 must have been what she was on during that last video. Jack asked how long this PT-141 stuff stays in the system, and the M.E. replied he had no idea. He told Jack he was not that familiar with the side effects or the complications, if any. Jack asked if there was anything or anyone they could talk to, who might know more. The M.E. stated he had called and left a message for a friend of his overseas to see what he could tell them about it. Jack asked what else they found from the items they took from Allison's home.

The M.E. stated there were lots of e-mails from Allison's computer that implicate her in all kinds of deception, lies; and some other e-mails show Allison was the one who sought out these guys to make these videos. Jack looked at each one of these e-mails carefully and read what Allison had written as well as what Heather and others had responded. Jack saw each time that Allison talked about how much money she was going to make in taking her clothes off. Jack saw the e-mails where Allison and Heather discussed a guy named Fred coming into the restaurant and talking to Allison about how much he liked seeing her in these videos. Jack also knew now Allison's boss was lying about his involvement with Allison. Jack read an e-mail where Allison talks about the busboy and how he was so hot for her as well.

As Jack read the e-mails and the replies from Heather, he knew she was up to her neck in deception, and now Jack understood why she did not want to tell him what happened. Jack also knew now that Heather had seen this Adam she and Allison refer to in e-mails on numerous days. He also knew that Heather and Allison had discussed Allison threatening Adam and Adam telling Allison she might wind up dead. Jack couldn't help but think Allison was way out of her league, and she was flirting with death making threats to some guy who was probably mobbed up. He just shook his head in disbelief. He knew he was going to have to take Heather in and get some true answers from her, no matter what her mother did regarding an attorney. Jack asked the M.E. if there had been any word regarding Allison's car or cell phone, but the M.E. told him he had no idea where either of those things were.

Jack was really hurt to find out all the things Allison was into. And now the whole community was going to know as well. Jack knew the press was going to get hold of this information, and when they do, all hell will break loose in this small town for this nice family. Jack went home after thanking the M.E. for this information.

Once Jack got into his car, he decided to go to the Tuttle's to let them know they could not make arrangements to bury their daughter until Allison's body could be released by the M.E.. Jack pulled up in front of the Tuttle's home about 9:00 p.m. and got out to start toward the front door when Paul opened it. Paul started toward the detective, and as the two men met on the walkway, Jack put his arm around Paul's shoulder and told him Allison's body had not been released by the medical examiner's office. Paul started to weep when Jennifer, Landon, and Lisa came out. Jack hugged each family member and told them they would be able to finally bury Allison very very soon. Then Paul asked if there had been any new progress in their daughter's investigation. Jack just remarked we are working on it. He left the Tuttle's and headed home for the day.

On Thursday morning as Jack was getting ready for work, he had so many things going through his mind he was having a hard time concentrating on the upcoming days' work. He just knew they still had to find this girl's vehicle as well as her cell phone. Jack decided he was going to talk to the girl's cell phone carrier and get her phone records by subpoena, if necessary. He felt her phone records would be a key to finding out who did this awful thing to her. He also still had what he felt were some key interviews with possibly the killer or one or more people who knew a lot more than they had been telling thus far. Jack left his house bound for the station to ask the district attorney in Forsyth County for permission to pick up the key suspects for questioning.

When Jack arrived at his office, the news media were waiting for him with lots of questions. Jack knew the evidence they had discovered would be leaked to the press by someone. He only stated to the press that this was an ongoing investigation, and he could not comment on any of the details. One of the reporters asked Jack if it was true Allison was on drugs.

Jack responded, "Have you people no shame? When we have answers we will let you know, and in the meantime don't print half-truths."

The reporter asked Jack what he was hiding, and he stopped in his tracks looking at the reporter and said, "We are not hiding anything. But if you want, I can arrest you for hindering prosecution. We have a large amount of suspects to rule out, and we need the press to work with us and not against us. We are asking all of you to work with us in this very serious matter. We are also asking anyone who has verifiable information about this case to contact us or crime stoppers immediately." Jack went on to say, "This family is going to bury their daughter, and we need to be respectful of this family in their time of despair. Thank you."

Jack went inside his office to speak with his team about any updates. The other members of Jack's team stated during the night that there had been nothing new. Jack called them all inside and then shut the door. He told them he wanted these people picked up and brought to the station for questioning. Jack also said he was through listening to bits and pieces of their stories, and he wanted them interrogated at great length about their role or part in this girl's death. Jack said each one of these people has lied to his face and it was about time they get to the bottom of their stories. At that point, Jack gave them a list of potential suspects or possible material witnesses. The list consisted of Chuck, Allison's boss; the father of the baby; the father's wife; John, the busboy; Michael, Allison's ex-boyfriend; Heather, Allison's friend; Chuck's wife; and the other waitresses at the restaurant.

Jack called the district attorney and told them what he was planning and that he needed the district attorney's help. Jack in the meantime went to see the other waitresses from the restaurant so he could see what they knew after they made the comments regarding Allison banging the boss.

Jack got to the restaurant at about 1:30 p.m. to speak with the ladies one at a time when Chuck came over and told him he was not going to pay these people to sit and talk to him. Jack told the owner he needed to stop interfering in police business. But Chuck got very belligerent, which indicated to Jack he was hiding something, so he got on his radio and asked for assistance. Chuck was making threats to Jack and stated he was tired of all this crap when Allison was nothing but a whore and got what she deserved.

In just a couple of minutes, several officers showed up, and Chuck was told he was being arrested at which point he started fighting with the officers. The officers placed Chuck on the floor and placed him in handcuffs. Chuck was lead to one of the cruisers and taken to jail for threatening a police officer. While the other officers took Chuck to jail Jack sat back down to complete the interviews with the other wait staff.

Jack was speaking to each one of the waitresses regarding the comments they made about Allison, and they told Jack that the way Chuck and Allison carried on made it pretty clear he was having sex with Allison. Jack asked them to be more specific, and the ladies went on to say Allison would show up late for work, and she would go into Chuck's office and stay there for several minutes and sometimes half an hour only to come out fixing her clothing. And the waitresses remembered one time when Allison came out zipping up the back of her dress.

Jack asked them about the busboy, John, and the waitresses just said he is a jerk on a good day, and he and Allison were at one another's throats all the time. They said Allison and John would curse one another in front of the customers, and Chuck did nothing to stop it. Jack asked about these new customers and if they knew a man named Fred. Both waitresses told Jack that Allison took care of these people and wanted no one else to speak to them. Jack thanked them both for their information. He was going to speak to John but decided he'd wait until he was brought to the station for the interview.

When Jack arrived back at the station, he checked in with his team to see if there were any updates. One member of Jack's team advised him they had gotten a copy of Allison's cell phone bill and had also asked the cell phone provider to locate her phone. The cell phone company stated the phone was not on the service anymore. The investigator asked the company how that was possible and they replied that the phone had to have been destroyed. The investigator asked if the phone was possibly just turned off, and the company told him the phone being off would not prevent it from showing up on their location service. They stated the only way it could have disappeared from the locator was to have been destroyed. So the chip can't be located.

Jack took a look at the cell phone records from Allison's phone. He saw text messages from several people: Heather, several other girls from her school, her mom and dad, and from an unknown phone number. Jack also noticed there were some other phone calls to Landon, but he felt like this was just normal activity. Jack was very interested in both Heather and the unknown numbers. Heather referenced this Adam person, and she had stated to Allison she was crazy for risking everything with someone she didn't even know. Allison had said to Heather she was thinking about telling Adam she would turn him into the police if he didn't take down the website. One of the unknown numbers replied not to threaten this person since threats usually result in someone getting hurt. Allison made a few other remarks then the same number told Allison that stupid people wind up getting dead. Jack thought to himself this was probably the person who may have killed Allison. Jacked asked his team to run down this number and see who it is assigned to. Jack also asked if the district attorney's office had issued the warrants he had asked for and was told they had not as yet.

Jack then turned his interest to Heather's other remarks. Heather and Allison seemed to be making up over some type of argument. Jack sat there for some time reviewing all text messages, thinking that Allison was so confused about all that was going on. She was in so far over her head, all she could see was the money she was going to receive. When Jack was through with the texts, he went home for the day.

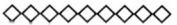

On Friday morning, Jack awakened to the news that led with a story about Allison Tuttle and her checkered life. The reporter was adamant about Allison's lifestyle and how a source told him the police were covering up for Allison and her extensive drug use. Jack was fighting mad with this loose cannon and called their station immediately. Jack demanded to speak to this reporter's immediate supervisor and started yelling at this person since this type of news coverage not only jeopardizes their investigation, but it taints this family with information that has not yet been verified.

The supervisor stated they had gotten information from a reliable source who they refused to name that Allison was on drugs. Jack stopped them right there and said, "Did it ever occur to you that she may not have taken them voluntarily? You were so concerned on getting your story on the air before anything else you failed to stop and verify your story before you recklessly ran with it."

The supervisor told Jack they were not trying to jeopardize his investigation, but the public has a right to know.

Jack then responded, "You don't think the public is entitled to a true story?" Jack went on to say he hoped the television station was prepared to retract this story if they find out these drugs were not taken voluntarily and also hoped they were prepared for the lawsuit that would follow. Finally, Jack told the supervisor he need not ever count on the police department to give his station the heads up on any story going forward; he just burned that bridge. Jack hung up the phone at that point.

Jack called his team, who just finished watching this bogus television story. He told his team they have to do everything possible to prove this television station and this reporter to be wrong, and they have to eat those words. The team told Jack during the night the people on his interview list had been brought down to the station for questioning. Jack was very happy to hear the district attorney decided to act on these people so they could get some answers.

Jack hurried getting ready so he could get to the station and begin the interviews. He decided to speak to Chuck's wife, Rachael, first since he knew Chuck was already in jail after being arrested on Thursday. Jack and one of the other investigators went in to see Rachael. Jack began by asking her if she wanted any coffee or water, and she declined. She asked what she was even doing here and why in the world had they arrested her husband. Jack explained he was sure she had heard about the death of Allison Tuttle, and Rachael stated she had heard about the girl's death.

Jack then told Rachael they were asking questions from numerous people who may know something about the girl's death. Rachael stated she barely even heard of the girl, so she certainly knew nothing about her death. He asked Rachael if she had ever met Allison, and she said, "Maybe once at the restaurant." Then he asked if her husband did not explain when he called her from jail. Rachael told Jack she found out through one of the waitresses from the restaurant that she assumed Chuck was not allowed any telephone calls. The other investigator told Rachael that Chuck had in fact made a phone call when he was arrested, but he was unsure who Chuck called. Jack told her he would have naturally thought Chuck had called her. All three of them just sat there for a second, wondering why he would not have called his wife and then whom did he call. Jack asked the other investigator to see if he could find out who Chuck called, and the investigator left the room.

Jack told Rachael about the incident at the restaurant and advised that Chuck was arrested for communicating a threat against a police officer. She told Jack her husband had been under a lot of pressure lately, and she had noticed a change in his behavior over the last several weeks. Jack asked what kind of behavior, and Rachael told him her husband had been very angry over the least little thing and had become distant in their relationship. Jack asked if there was something wrong, perhaps with the business, and she replied Chuck takes care of that stuff. She then told Jack she still did not understand why he thought she might know something about the girl's death. Jack asked her if Chuck had ever been unfaithful to her. Rachael told Jack that was none of his business. Jack told her he had overheard a conversation at the restaurant between two of the waitresses who made accusations her husband was possibly having an affair with another woman.

Rachael stood up and told Jack she was not going to sit there and listen to these accusations about her husband. About that time, the other investigator came back into the room and whispered to Jack that Chuck had called one of the other waitresses to get him out of jail. She was told there was no bail on Chuck until he appeared before a judge. Jack then told Rachael what he had just been told, and she just sat back down in the chair in disbelief. Rachael stated she knew something was wrong. She then said, "He promised me this would never happen again."

Jack said to Rachael, "So he has done this before."

She confirmed he had done this before with someone else, but he had promised it was just a one-time thing. Rachael then looked at Jack and said, "So now I get it, you're telling me he was screwing this Allison."

Jack told her he has all suspicions he was at least hitting on her, but as far as having sex, he would know more after he had spoken to Chuck. Jack then told her if she would be willing to stay in the room while they question her husband, which will perhaps give them a better understanding about this whole situation. Rachael told Jack she would have a coffee, light with two sugars. Jack asked the other investigator to please get her coffee and make her comfortable.

Jack went into the interrogation room where Chuck was sitting. When he walked in, Chuck made a comment about how he was sorry for getting so mad at the restaurant yesterday. Jack thanked him and then asked why he thought he had gotten so angry. Chuck told Jack his wife had been ragging on him to spend more time with her and not so much at the restaurant. Jack asked Chuck his wife's name, and he replied Rachael. He asked him how their marriage was doing, and Chuck told him pretty well except his wife didn't trust him and was forever accusing him of having affairs. Chuck assured Jack nothing like that had ever happened before.

Jack stood there ringing his hands while Chuck was telling him this story. Jack asked Chuck, "But you've never cheated on her?"

"No," Chuck said. "Rachael is good to me."

Jack told Chuck about the conversation he had overheard at the restaurant.

Chuck responded, "These bitches are always all up in someone else's business."

Jack looked at Chuck and said, "So they were right?"

"No, I meant they always think they know what someone else is doing. It's none of their business what I do."

Jack looked at Chuck and told him he sounded like a man having an affair. Jack told him he had also spoken to someone who had seen Allison coming out of his office fixing her clothing and even zipping up her dress.

Chuck said, "That's a lie that never happened."

"What if I was to tell you we know for a fact you cheated on your wife with another woman. What would you say then?"

Chuck told Jack he did not know what he was talking about.

Then Jack told Chuck, "See that window?"

Chuck responded yes.

"Your wife is on the other side, and she heard everything you said. Want me to bring her in?"

Chuck told Jack he too was a liar that his wife was not there. About that time the door opened and another investigator brought in Rachael. She was screaming at the top of her lungs. "You lying bastard. You did have an affair with another woman, and you know it. Now you're screwing this sixteen-year-old girl. I hope they put you away forever."

Chuck said, "Baby, I love you."

Rachael told him to go to hell. And the investigator took her out.

Rachael went back into the other room while Jack was still talking to Chuck. Rachael was very emotional and was crying and then screaming about how stupid she was for staying with this loser. The other investigator asked Rachael if he had other affairs, and she confirmed he had been with other women, not just the one she told Jack about. He asked her why she stayed with him and she said, "I'm a fool, that's why."

He asked her what she was going to do now, and she responded with a big sigh, "I thought this time was going to be different."

He inquired what had happened last time. She told him Chuck had become obsessed with this woman where Rachael had worked. He asked where she had worked, and she told him she was a personal assistant for a corporate executive. The investigator asked her why she left. Rachael told him, "I didn't like the way he treated me, like I was a piece of meat and not his assistant." He asked if this guy had ever forced her to have relations with him. She stated he had gotten her alone a few times, and she barely made it out of the office without having to call the police. She went on to say she had met Chuck in a bar, and he seemed to be really sweet, and they started to hit it off, then got married. Shortly after their marriage, he cheated on her with one of his old girlfriends. She said he promised not to do it again, and for a while he didn't. And then it happened again with the same woman and then with another woman. The investigator asked her why she stayed with this man. Rachael said, "I loved him. But now looking back, it wasn't my finest hour." He asked her if she was going to be all right, and Rachael said, "Know any good divorce lawyers?" He stated he was sure she was going to be fine. She asked if she could go. So after speaking to Jack, the investigator let Rachael leave.

While this conversation was going on, Jack and Chuck were still talking in the other room. Chuck asked Jack why his wife was there anyway. Jack told him they were talking to anyone who might have known Allison, and also they wanted to ask her if you had ever been unfaithful. He said, "Now see what you've done. You've ruined my marriage."

Jack laughed and said, "Hey, pal, you ruined your own marriage." Jack asked for Chuck to be returned to his cell to await arraignment next week before a judge.

Jack asked where Michael was being held for his interview. He went into the room and asked Michael if he knew why he was there. Michael started by saying the only reason he was there was because he dated Allison. He went on to say that the entire time he dated her, she was nothing but a pain in the butt. He said everything that happened was always his fault. Jack asked Michael why the two of them broke up. Michael said Allison always wanted things he could not buy for her. Jack asked what kinds of things, and Michael answered, "Expensive jewelry, expensive clothes, pretty much anything normal people can't afford." Jack then asked him if he ever bought Allison any of these things, and Michael stated he had bought her a few pieces of jewelry, but nothing of the caliber she wanted. Jack asked him to describe the jewelry he had bought for Allison. After Michael described some of the jewelry, Jack asked him if he saw a photo of the jewelry could he identify any of the pieces. Michael said he would try. So Jack got a photo of the jewelry piece they had found in the dumpster and brought it back into the interview room along with some jewelry from other investigations. Michael looked at the photos and immediately saw the piece he had given Allison. It was a pair of earrings with turquoise stones. Jack told him Allison was found with one of these earrings but not the other. Michael was actually happy that Allison at least still had the earrings.

Jack started asking Michael about the nasty things he had said to Allison. Michael replied he was very upset at the way Allison had treated him in front of their classmates. Jack asked what she said, and Michael told him she had said she would rather go out with an animal than to go out with him. Michael added all she had to do was say no, but instead, she chose to embarrass him in front of people they both knew. Jack told him he understood how awkward that must have been.

Michael told Jack he had no idea how cold she could be and how, when they did go out, she flirted with every man she saw. He said if she saw a man with a nice car or wearing jewelry, she would make a point of trying to make eye contact with the man. Jack said, "Well, in her case, it would be young men."

Michael told Jack she flirted with all ages of men, and it didn't matter if they were married or with someone. Jack started to think how that piece of information might fit into the puzzle. Jack asked Michael if he had noticed other things about Allison and her likes and dislikes. Michael asked why, and Jack went on to say that the more he could find out from people who went out with Allison and knew her personally, it might help solve this mystery. Michael told Jack about her love for having her picture taken and how she dreamed about being a movie star.

Jack asked Michael if he would mind his taping the conversation, and Michael agreed. Jack told him he had to ask this question: "Did you hurt Allison in any way at any time?" Michael stated he had never touched her in a way to hurt her. Jack asked if they had been sexually active and asked him to be honest. Michael stated they had sex a few times, but Allison wanted to do freaky things he was not comfortable with. Jack asked what kinds of things, and Michael explained all the positions and toys she wanted to use, which was one of the reasons they broke up. Jack asked him to explain, and he said Allison wanted to use sex toys and have him stick them in places they don't belong. Jack thanked him for being honest.

He asked Michael if he ever remembered seeing Allison wearing any diamond earrings. Michael told him he had not only seen her wearing them; he knew she had other pieces of jewelry in her locker at school. Jack looked confused and told Michael the police had searched her locker and found none of those things. Michael said she was forever letting other girls she knew borrow them. Jack asked for the girl's names, and Michael gave him several names. He told Jack she had clothes and jewelry she gave to Heather to hide at her home. Jack then was thinking back to the time he went to Heather's home and her mother not wanting Heather to answer any questions.

Jack could not wait until this interview was over so he could get to speak with Heather. Jack asked Michael what else he knew about Allison and if Allison had ever posed for photos to publish or posed for a video. Michael responded she had gone to those Glamour Shots places and had fancy pictures made. Michael was asked if he had any of these photos, and he said he did not. Michael stated he had seen Allison dancing in a video that some friend of Allison's had made a while back. Jack asked where he saw it, and he stated on the Internet. Jack asked if he remembered the site, and Michael said he thought he still had the Internet site written down at home. Jack asked what she was wearing, and Michael said it was just in some short shorts and a tank top. Jack asked Michael to get the address to him as soon as possible, and he said he would. Jack told Michael he was free to leave.

At 5:00 p.m. on Friday afternoon, as Jack headed to do the interview with Heather, he got a telephone call from a detective in Mecklenburg County, North Carolina, saying a vehicle registered to Mr. Paul Tuttle was found abandoned at the Douglas International Airport in Charlotte, NC. The detective went on to say the vehicle was parked in their long-term parking lot sometime on Saturday after Allison had gone missing. The detective also mentioned they had not performed any forensic testing since Jack was the lead detective. Jack thanked the detective and told him someone from his office would be in touch to pick up the vehicle for transport back to his area.

Jack spoke to his forensic people as well as his other team members and advised them of the information he had just gotten from the Charlotte detective. Jack asked them to get the team together and do the forensic tests at the holding facility in Charlotte, rather than chance losing any DNA evidence, bringing it back here. One of the forensic team investigators told Jack that since it was so late in the day, they would go to Charlotte on Friday morning. Jack replied back, "That's a great plan, but you're leaving in an hour. Have a safe trip." Jack was excited the vehicle was finally found and was looking forward to getting the information from the vehicle itself. The one thing that puzzled Jack was why the car was left in Charlotte and if the killer was from that area.

Jack walked into the interrogation room where Heather and her mom were supposed to be waiting, but when he opened the door, the room was empty. Jack went back out of the room asking, "Where the heck is Heather?" One of his team told him Heather's mother was very upset over being held all day, saying that the next time they want to speak to her daughter, to get a warrant. Jack called the district attorney's office and spoke to one of the assistants and advised the person he needed a material witness warrant issued for Heather, and he needed it immediately. The assistant told him there was no way they were going to find a judge at 6:00 p.m. willing to give them a warrant. Jack told the assistant that the girl's information was crucial to solving the case, and the girl may be getting rid of evidence. The assistant asked Jack if he was sure the girl has the evidence or was the information just hearsay from another party. Jack had to admit he was told this girl has potential evidence, so he had no choice except to wait until Monday.

Jack saw he had gotten a message from the M.E.'s office advising him Allison's body was released and could now be laid to rest. Jack called the Tuttle family to give them the heads up so they could make arrangements to bury Allison.

On Saturday morning, when Jack woke up to start the day, he turned on the television to a story that was already playing. As Jack sat near the television, he saw a reporter standing outside the Tuttle home doing a story about the Allison Tuttle murder. This reporter was saying it had been several days since the girl had been found dead, and there were no arrests in this murder. Then the reporter stated they had gotten a tip from a reliable source that the medical examiner's office was doing a postmortem viability test on the fetus of Allison Tuttle's baby. The reporter stated that Allison being four weeks pregnant was not known to the public. Jack was furious with this news station; releasing information which was not only partially false, but it was giving confidence to the killer that they would never be brought to justice.

Jack got dressed and went down to the local television station, asking to see the person in charge. When Jack got to sit down with the producer, he shouted his displeasure with this type of journalism. The producer said they had an obligation to report the news. Jack stated they did not have an obligation to embarrass the family and hinder the investigation. He stated they were not ready to release this information for fear the father of the baby might flee the area, making it even harder to find this person. Jack asked the producer if this was the story he would like to see someone run if it were his daughter. The producer agreed not to run a story without Jack's input going forward. Jack thanked the producer and promised him that when they had valid information, he would release it to his station only. The producer told Jack he was hopeful the person or persons would be found and prosecuted. Jack told the producer they had found Allison's vehicle with the assistance of another law enforcement agency and that his team was there at this time gathering forensic evidence. The producer was thankful to Jack for sharing that information. Jack and the producer shook hands, and Jack left the station.

When Jack got back into his cruiser, he called his team and asked what they had found in Allison's vehicle. The investigator he spoke to said that the left-side door had been brushed by another vehicle, seemingly the same as running someone off the road. He also stated the rear bumper of the car had been bumped like someone was trying to cause her to crash. The investigator went on to say that Allison's cell phone was in the floor of the car under the seat, which indicated she may have been using it when the impact happened. He then said they had found lots of fingerprints in and around the car, and it appeared the girl had been held in the trunk as they found traces of the same duct tape that was used on her hands and mouth. He added they found the matched earring to the one found in the dumpster. Jack asked if they found her purse, and the investigator told him there was no purse. Jack asked if there was any blood found in the car, and he stated no blood, but they did find traces of some type of grease. The investigator told Jack they will know a lot more after getting some of these things back to the lab. Jack told them to get the car back here as quickly as they could and told them all to be careful coming back home.

During the day on Saturday, Jack went back to his office to go through every piece of evidence, again feeling like they may have missed something. As Jack sat in his office, mulling over all of the interviews and the pieces of evidence, he got to thinking about this town and its past. Jack started writing on a board things he wanted to bring to the forefront.

- John
- Father of Allison's baby
- Wives of Allison's lovers
- Two men from restaurant
- Heather
- Video list
- Photographer
- Adam
- Other girl from video
- Kidnapper
- Chuck
- DNA fetus test due October 26

Jack felt as though these were the key players in the death of Allison. He kept thinking some part of the news story was right; they really don't have a key suspect as yet, but then there have been more distractions than on a normal investigation. He sat there staring at the board, thinking back to one of the interviews. He thought about something Chuck had said or actually didn't say. When Rachael was yelling at Chuck and accused him of "screwing this sixteen-year-old girl," he never denied that statement; instead he just said "baby, I love you." Jack thought why would he not have denied it if it wasn't going on. So he went back to his list and added Chuck's name.

Jack also thought back to Michael's interview and his mentioning a friend of Allison's who took the video but never saying who that was. Jack made a note to ask Michael when he will call him about the website of the video of Allison.

Jack decided to stop by the convenience store about 6:00 p.m. where they had found Allison's body to see the son-in-law who was on duty when the girl was found. Jack arrived at the store and went inside and started speaking to the owner's son-in-law. Jack asked what time he came in to work on that Friday, and he stated he came to work at 4:00 p.m. and was scheduled to work until 2:00 a.m., Saturday. Jack asked if he saw anyone coming in the store during that time frame who didn't seem to fit in or seemed to be out of place. The man just said he couldn't remember anything specific about any person on that shift. Jack then asked if he saw any vehicle going around to the back of the building, and the man said there were always cars going behind the building. He said, "Have you seen the people who come in this store? Nothing but drunks and dope heads." The man went on to say, "All I keep my eye on are the thugs that come in here, otherwise they steal you blind."

Jack asked him if he took out the trash anytime that shift, and the man told him he does not take the trash out after dark because of the neighborhood, and he doesn't want to get robbed. Jack then asked if the store had ever been robbed, and the man said it had been in the past. He asked when the last time was, and the man said about a month ago. Jack asked him if he remembered the person or persons who robbed the store. The man just shook his head no. Jack asked, "You know a lot more than you are telling me. Are you lying to me?"

The man stated he didn't want these guys to come after him.

Jack said, "We can protect you from these people if you just tell me the truth."

"These guys might kill me."

Jack asked if he could recognize them if he saw them again. He said, "Yes." He told the man to come to his office on Monday to look at some mug shots. He said he would. Jack went home for the day.

Jack had been so busy with all that has been going on he had not even checked his messages. When Jack checked his messages he found Paul Tuttle had called him telling Jack the funeral was scheduled for Sunday October 13 and the viewing was scheduled for tonight from 7pm to 9pm at the local funeral home. Jack was in a rush to get to the funeral home since it was already almost 7pm. Jack asked one of his team to release John the busboy and have him come back for the interview on Monday.

Jack took off in a flash to make it to the funeral home not only for the family and the town, but to see if anyone showed up at the viewing who either seemed out of place or did not look familiar. Jack entered the funeral home that was already packed with people paying their respects. Jack hugged each one of Allison's family and just blended in with the locals so he could just watch who came and left. He carefully watched each person as they came down the line to see their reaction when they saw the body and the family.

Five hundred people came and went, which was very normal; and some of the people were crying as they reached the coffin, which was expected. Jack noticed a few people who seemed to have a strange reaction when they looked at the family, and he made notes of the names and the people, most of whom he knew, just in case he wanted to speak with them over the next few days. The time was now after

8:00 p.m., and neither Heather nor her mom had made an appearance, which Jack found to be quite odd. Jack was speaking to one of the family when a man he did not recognize entered the funeral home. The man slowly approached the family as he spoke to each one, and then Jack noticed him weeping as he got closer to Allison.

Once the man left the coffin and started toward the door to leave, Jack approached him and asked him for his name. The man looked at Jack and asked why he was interested, so Jack showed the man his badge. The man gave Jack his name, and he wrote it in his notebook. Jack asked the man how he had come to know Allison, and the man stated he was a customer at the restaurant where Allison worked. Jack asked how he came to be a customer at the restaurant since he had not seen the man in the town before. The man told him he was visiting his family in the area, and they recommended the restaurant as a place to dine. Jack asked the man the name of his family, and the man stated he had answered all the questions he felt comfortable with and left. Jack wrote down the model and make of vehicle the man was driving and then got the license plate number. He went inside and asked Paul if he remembered seeing the man, and Paul was so distraught he was unsure.

Jack couldn't help but think that was such a strange reaction to have from someone who was just visiting the area. He thought this man must have known her from somewhere else or some other time in their lives. Jack spoke to Jennifer about the man, but she too was too upset to focus on the man he was referring to. Jack paid his respects again to the family just before he left the funeral home and promised to be at the funeral on Sunday.

Jack got into his cruiser and asked the National Crime Information Center (NCIC) to look up the man's license plate number to see who this guy was. The information came back, and Jack had the information for this stranger who turned out not to be so much of a stranger after all. Jack got out of the cruiser and went back inside the funeral home to find Paul. Once Jack found Paul, he told him he now knew the identity of the man he asked him about. Jack said the name the man had given him turned out to be false. He said he checked the database, and the man was Tony Bolero. Paul looked at Jack and asked if he was sure. Jack stated he got the information from the man's license plate and called it into NCIC.

Paul said, "I didn't even recognize him. I haven't seen him for like ten years."

Jack stated this Tony Bolero went away for child pornography.

Paul said, "He used to live near us, and he was brought up on charges for child pornography on school children in the area." Jack asked how he knew Allison, and Paul stated he had been involved with schoolchildren in her school at the time. Jack asked what this person's role in Allison's life was, and Paul told him he was Allison's bus driver when she was in the first grade. Jack asked if he had ever been alone with Allison, and Paul just said Allison was the last person on the bus every day. Then Paul asked, "What are you implying?"

Jack said he was just asking a question.

Paul said, "I never believed he did such a thing."

Jack said, "He went away for the crime that speaks volumes as to his guilt."

Paul asked again what Jack was implying, and Jack just said, "I am a cop, and it's my job to be suspicious." Jack asked Paul if he found it odd this man would be at the funeral home after only knowing Allison for such a short time. Paul just shook his head.

Jack couldn't help but wonder why this man, who was Allison's bus driver, would show up at the funeral home after not seeing her in years. Jack was thinking that a criminal might have just shown up here out of the blue, for no other reason than having known this girl, using visiting a relative as an excuse. It seemed very strange he would just happen to be in town when Allison turned up missing and stayed around long enough to be at her funeral. Jack decided to check on the address given on the Bolero NCIC check, and the exact location given was an address that would put his home in the middle of a river in Virginia. Jack made a note to check with his parole officer on Monday to see if he has a current address. Jack was tired after a long day and went home to go to bed.

On Sunday morning, October 13, Detective Jack woke up early and went through his usual routine of eating breakfast and showering. Finally, he went outside to get his newspaper off the curb, and as he was walking back up to the house, he opened the paper to see huge headlines that read "Tuttle's Funeral Today." Jack was like Tuttle's, and then he started reading the story that went on to say Allison and her baby were being buried today at the cemetery adjoining the church where her father is the pastor. The article did not paint a very good light on Allison or the Tuttle family.

This investigative reporter wrote about how Paul shouted in the restaurant that he was ashamed of his daughter and she was not going to ruin him. Also how Jennifer had been in trouble with the law in her earlier years. The article also told about Jennifer's loose past with young men and the number of young men she used to "hang out with." The reporter started with all of Allison's so-called friends, who were quick to say she was flirty with all kinds of men. There were statements in the article regarding Allison's endless list of potential fathers for her baby. Jack was really embarrassed for the Tuttle family and everything they were going through now, let alone all these rumors flying around. Jack couldn't help but wonder what the church community must be thinking about their pastor and his family.

Jack got into his car and drove over to the Tuttle's house to see if he could be of any assistance with the press. When Jack turned the corner, there were wall-to-wall news-media vehicles from all over the state, not just in the area. Jack stopped his cruiser and told the newspeople they had to back off the lawn and give these people some room. The news media then turned on Jack, quizzing him about the investigation and when they would be arresting the murderer. Jack stated, "This is an ongoing investigation, and I am not in a position to comment, other than to say we are getting closer to an arrest any day." He then excused himself and rang the doorbell to the Tuttle home and went inside.

Once Jack entered the house, he was bombarded with all kinds of accusations about the news story. Jack assured the family that these people didn't get any of this news from their investigation. He advised the family to be realistic, and information like this was not going to be secret for very long. Jack told the family, "These people can get information out of people whom even the police can't get sometimes." He went on to say that just the hint of improper activities is going to get their blood boiling. Paul asked Jack how he should handle this, and he replied, "The best you can." Jack then told Paul the more they try to hide information, the more they are going to pick the bones.

Jennifer said, "They made me look like a tramp."

Jack said, "Everyone has something in their past they would rather keep hidden. But sometimes, it just gets out." He added, "Just tell it like it is." Jack asked Paul if they could have a word. The two men walked into the other room.

Jack asked if everything was all right, and Paul told him he was afraid of what he might find out about Jennifer and Allison. Jack told him he was a good man, and he loved his family. Jack told Paul he would find a way to handle any situation. Paul just said, "Jack, I have to bury my daughter today and a grandchild I never even met."

"You'll do this with dignity just like the rest of your life."

They walked back in the other room.

When the two men reentered, Landon asked what that was all about and why did it have to be a secret. Jack explained he wanted to speak with his dad regarding the funeral. Then Landon asked what all these lies were regarding their mother. Jack told the family he was going into another room while they had a family meeting. Jack left the family alone so the kids could understand the explanations from their parents regarding all of the rumors and stories.

As Jack walked into another room, there was someone ringing the doorbell, and he shouted out he would get the door. When Jack opened the door, he was met by several reporters so he escorted them off the property and told them that if they came back, he would have them arrested. Jack turned around and went back inside the home.

Jack settled into the living room while he waited for the family to come out of their meeting. While he was sitting there alone, he kept thinking that the conversations going on in the other room had to be so intense. After an hour, the family reappeared in tears but holding one another's hands, asking God to stand by them in this time of need and despair. Jack waited for the family to make the first comment. Paul and Jennifer held one another tightly and told Jack there was nothing on this earth going to break up their family. They had agreed to stand by one another and to stand by Allison and the baby. Jack told the family he knew they would come out the other side as a family. They smiled and just said, "We are going to answer questions from the press and put some of these rumors to bed." Jack told them he thought that was a very good idea, and he would support their decision. Jack walked alongside the family as they approached the news reporters.

Paul wanted to speak, but the reporters were like vultures and wanted to speak over one another, so Jack stepped in and said, "These people are going through one of the most difficult days they have ever faced in their lives. If you act civilized, they will want to answer your questions. If not, they will walk away and go back into the house." The news media began to settle down and let Paul point to the reporters one by one to answer their specific questions.

The first reporter asked Paul about Allison being pregnant and if he knew who the father of the baby was. Paul answered, "It's not my place to judge her or her choices. God will be the judge in this situation. I can tell you this. No one in this family knows anything about who the father might be."

Paul then pointed to another reporter, who asked if he was aware of the number of men Allison had been hanging around. He then answered, "I have no idea of the number of friends Allison had, and until I have factual information, I can't comment on that either."

Paul pointed to yet another reporter, who asked what he thought about what Jennifer had done in her earlier years. Paul handled it very well by saying, "I would have to imagine there is not one person here, including all of you, who wouldn't mind telling us all of your secrets including your drug use in college. Are there? I am not my wife's judge. I am her husband, and I have no right to analyze anything she had done before I met her. The only thing important to me is all the great things she has done since I have known her."

Paul then pointed to another reporter, who asked what Landon and Lisa felt about all of these rumors and stories. Landon approached the microphones and said, "My sister

Lisa and I don't think it's our place to judge anyone especially my sister, who is not here to defend herself."

Paul then came back to the microphones and stated they were getting ready to start the funeral in a few minutes and thanked the press for their time. Jack put his arms around the family and told Paul he did great with the reporters. Jack said, "Paul, you were like a politician. You answered the questions without telling them anything."

About 2:00 p.m., the guests and the family arrived outside of the church and began to file inside. The chapel was beautiful with gorgeous flowers flowing over the sides of the containers. The lighting was perfect, and the music was softly playing in the background. At the front of the church, right in front of the stage, was Allison's coffin. The dark oak coffin with gold handles was beautifully shined and held the body of the Tuttles' oldest daughter and her fetus. Paul was on stage, and while the organist played, he just sat in his chair, thinking of the eulogy he was about to give. After twenty minutes, the church was full of mourners made up of family, friends, and classmates.

Paul stood up and asked the congregation to bow their heads in prayer. Paul asked for the Lord's forgiveness for all of those who came here today only to cast dispersions on the truth and make up stories and rumors about things they knew nothing about. He asked the Lord to watch over his daughter and her baby and protect them in heaven. Paul thanked all the people who took time to be with them in their time of need. He choked up when he started to speak about Allison's childhood and how she was his little girl. He talked about her with her hair in curlers trying to be like her mom when she was three years old. Paul asked the congregation not to judge their daughter but rather wait until the entire truth comes out and to keep his family in their prayers and to hug their children a little closer tonight before they go to bed.

Paul said on behalf of his family to not judge your children but rather love them no matter what. He asked them to be open to their children and let them know they could speak to their parents about any subject and to be open to their other family members as well. Paul stated that the criminals who had done this to his daughter and grandchild will be caught since Detective Jack Williams was the one after them. Then Paul asked the entire congregation to sing a variety of songs that were Allison's favorites. The pallbearers went to the front of the church to prepare to carry out the casket.

The casket was then carried out the doors and into the cemetery, where mourners who wanted to go to the burial surrounded the cemetery plot. Jack made sure the reporters stayed back away from the grave itself. Paul tried to ask for a prayer but broke down, and one of the deacons took over. Once the prayer was over, the deacon read a scripture from the Bible that meant something to Allison. The deacon then asked the family to come put a flower on the casket of their family member and loved ones.

One by one, each one came by and placed a flower on Allison's casket. Some of the family members would whisper something to her, and some were just weeping. Finally, the deacon led everyone in a prayer. The family was escorted back into the limousine to take them back to their home. The reporters all went their own way after trying to get final photo shots of the family members as they got into the limo. Jack stayed behind to make sure no one was doing anything that shouldn't be done. Jack's team walked up next to him and asked if he was all right since they knew this was personal for their boss. Jack responded he was fine, but they had to solve this case and make this entire thing mean something. After everyone had left, except for the grave diggers, Jack and his team left to go home.

Jack arrived back home at about 6:30 p.m. only to find an envelope under his front doormat. He was surprised someone had gone to the trouble to find out where he lived or followed him home. He took the envelope and walked inside. Once inside, Jack was very careful with the envelope as his first concern was fingerprints on it and not to disturb them. He took a letter opener and split the top of the envelope so he could get the contents out. Jack had even put on cotton gloves so as not to wipe off any fingerprints.

The envelope contained photos of Allison posing in very compromising positions, wearing very seductive outfits. On the back of one of the pictures was a handwritten note, saying "my personal favorite." Jack wondered who dropped these off and for what reason. Was it to bring attention to these photos? Was it to throw Jack off some trail? Was this to make Allison look even worse? Or was it to make Jack think she was now some porno star or something? Someone went to a lot of trouble to bring these to Jack's attention. Jack couldn't wait to get these to the lab to see whose prints were on these things or if they were wiped clean. Jack just could not understand why someone thought these were so important. He wondered why a person wouldn't just mail them to the station. The first person Jack thought of who might bring these to his home was Tony Bolero or someone who worked for him.

On Monday morning, Detective Jack got ready for work and was eager to start the day. He was looking forward to getting the convenience store clerk to look at the mug books and to get the information from Allison's car. He was also looking forward to doing the interview with John and get information from the photos left at his door. And lastly, he was hoping the district attorney was going to let them bring Heather in for her avoidance from giving information and having information as a material witness. It was certainly going to be a full day with hopefully positive results.

Jack arrived at his office and went inside, giving the envelope to his team very carefully to preserve any fingerprints. The envelope had the photos Jack saw and he asked them to get to work on any fingerprints. Jack went into his office. Then one of his team came in, giving him the results of the fingerprints from Allison's vehicle. Jack was stunned to see the number of people who had fingerprints on this girl's car. There were thirty-two different sets of fingerprints, and of those, six had been fingerprinted before. Jack assumed that most of the other twenty-six were schoolmates or friends of the family. The six who had been fingerprinted were Landon Tuttle; Jennifer Tuttle; Tony Bolero a.k.a. Michael Matthews, a.k.a. Paul Thomas; John Gordon a.k.a. Rodney Jones, a.k.a. Jimmy Little, a.k.a. the busboy from the restaurant where Allison worked; Heather Gibson, Allison's friend from school; and the one person Jack never expected to see on this list, Ken Roberts, his stepdad.

Jack knew Tony Bolero was a long-time criminal and had served time in prison. Jack now knew how he was so familiar with John, the busboy from the restaurant. He must have seen a flier somewhere about a crime John had committed. Jack was wondering why these other people had been fingerprinted before and if they had been arrested for some other crime. He asked the investigator to see if he could find out what the reason was that the others were fingerprinted. Another investigator came in and told Jack, "John is here from the restaurant." Jack thanked him and went to the interview.

Jack asked one of the other investigators which room John was in. The first thing out of his mouth was, "Now I know where I know you from, and now I know you knew I would find out once I got you in here." Jack asked how he wanted to be addressed: John Gordon, Rodney Jones, or Jimmy Little.

John just looked at the detective and said, "I go by John."

Jack said, "I'm sure you do. I'm sure if I go see Chuck, he knows you as John Gordon, right?"

John said he admits he has had a run in with the law and that he needed a break so he used his uncle's name who passed away.

Jack asked John, "You wouldn't know anything about his death, would you?"

John said his uncle died from a heart attack and told Jack to check it out. John went on to say he had gotten picked up for stealing a bicycle when he was sixteen. And then another time when he was nineteen, he got caught with stolen merchandise. Jack asked if he stole the merchandise, and John said, "No, but I got caught with it." He was then asked if he wanted to confess anything, and he said, "About what, you think I killed that bitch? She was nothing but a prick teaser, and all she wanted was what she could get out of someone."

Jack said, "She and you argued in front of customers and other employees at the restaurant."

"That bitch wouldn't give me the time of day since I couldn't buy her the gifts other men gave her." Jack asked who, and John said, "Several guys came into the restaurant, and I heard them whispering to Allison about her website and her sexy body." Jack asked if he could identify these guys, and John said he could. Jack then asked why his fingerprints were found on Allison's car. John said, "Once, at the restaurant, I was outside just looking at her car, and I touched it." John told Jack that one of the guys giving her fancy gifts was her boss, Chuck. Jack said they had interviewed Chuck already. John said, "Did you look in Chuck's office? I've seen jewelry in his office that Allison wore." Jack told John to sit tight while he got John to look at the mug shot books. Jack left the room and asked another investigator to have John look at the mug books.

Jack went back to his office, and the clerk from the convenience store came in to also look at the mug books. One of Jack's team took John into one area and the clerk into another area. Just about the time Jack got started on another task, he had to go to the medical examiner's office, who called and asked him to stop by there later today. Jack was still preoccupied with seeing his stepdad's name on the list of people who had been fingerprinted before. Jack decided to call his mom, Linda, and talk with her a little bit while he was waiting for the two guys to finish looking through the books. Jack's mom was very happy to hear from him, and like most moms, she was asking why he had not been calling. So Jack explained with all that was going on with this big case; he had been so busy he had no time to call. Jack told his mom he didn't stop working most nights until late, and he was up early right back at it.

Before Jack got off the phone with his mom, he asked her if Ken, his stepdad, had ever been in any trouble with the law. Linda stated not that she was aware of and then asked why he would ask that. Jack just said his name came up in a conversation and just wondered if he had been in the past. When Jack got off the phone, there was a knock on his office door, and one of the investigators came in. The investigator told Jack that John had not seen anyone in the books that matched the people coming into the restaurant.

Jack went to check on the clerk to see if he had seen anyone he recognized from the books. He asked the clerk if he had found anyone in the books he had seen before at the store. The clerk had picked out a couple of guys he stated were part of a robbery in the store. Jack noted these guys and their records. One of the investigators escorted the clerk out of the building when the clerk told the investigator he just saw the third guy and the investigator asked where. The clerk pointed at John, who was leaving the building. The investigator got to Jack, telling him what the clerk had just said. The investigator asked Jack if he wanted him to run after John, but Jack told him not to.

The investigator walked up close to Jack and asked him why he let John go, and Jack stated, "We know where he is going." He then went on to say he wanted to look around in the restaurant and the owner's office, and this would give him probable cause to do so. Jack also asked if they had gotten the warrant to bring Heather in, but the investigator stated not yet. Jack told the investigator they were going to the restaurant to look for evidence.

Jack and the other investigator got to the restaurant, and they went inside to see Chuck. When Chuck saw the detectives, he said, "I'm through answering any more questions unless you've got a warrant." Jack told him, "You can answer a few questions here, or we can arrest you and shut down your restaurant while we search it from top to bottom." Chuck asked what they wanted. Jack stated that when he was at the station, there was a question he never answered. Chuck asked what it was, and Jack responded,

"You never did confirm or deny whether you were having sex with Allison."

Chuck said, "Why would I have sex with a sixteen year old?"

"That's not an answer."

Chuck then told Jack he had not had sex with Allison. Jack then asked Chuck if he would mind if they looked around the restaurant. Chuck asked what they were looking for.

"Is there anything in the restaurant that belongs to Allison?" Jack asked.

Chuck stated, "Not that I'm aware of."

"Then you won't mind us looking around, will you?"

Chuck told the men they could look around.

The two police looked in lockers to see what was there and then came upon a locker with a lock on it. Jack asked whose locker that was, and Chuck stated he was not sure.

Jack asked, "Do we have permission to look in the locker?"

Chuck said, "What if I say no?"

"We'll get a search warrant and look anyway."

Chuck agreed to let the men look but claimed he could not find the key. Jack told the other investigator to get the bolt cutter out of the car.

After getting the bolt cutter, they cut off the lock. Jack put on gloves and started looking at everything in it. The contents consisted of a work dress from the restaurant, a few T-shirts for the guys working in the restaurant, and a metal box. Jack opened the box. When he saw some jewelry, he asked Chuck who that belonged to.

Chuck said, "I'm hiding it here until my wife's birthday."

Jack asked when her birthday was, and Chuck said it will be next month, which would have been October.

Jack said, "That's funny. Your wife told me her birthday was in March." Jack took out all of the jewelry and examined each piece carefully. He was no jeweler, but he estimated the value of the jewelry to be several thousand dollars.

Jack asked Chuck if he had the receipt for this jewelry, and Chuck stated he did not know where it was.

Jack told Chuck, "This jewelry could be from a robbery, for all we know. We will take photos of the jewelry and give you a receipt for the items, then we'll see if any of this is stolen."

Chuck then said, "You can't do that. This is my jewelry."

"You have a felon working at this restaurant, and since you could not tell me whose locker this was, for all I know, this jewelry could be stolen."

Chuck asked who the felon was.

Jack replied, "Your busboy, I'm sure he can explain it. He was identified as a robber of the convenience store where Allison's body was found."

Jack and the other investigator went over to John and arrested him for robbing the convenience store. Jack told

John they had a positive identification. John swore he didn't do any robbery, but Jack just said, "Tell it to a judge."

The other investigator took the prisoner out to the cruiser while Jack took pictures of all the jewelry and wrote out a receipt for Chuck. Jack exited the restaurant and got into the cruiser to go back to the station with their prisoner.

Once Jack and the other investigator got back to the station, they placed John in a holding cell until transportation officers could pick up their prisoner and take him to jail.

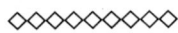

It was getting late in the day on Monday, and Jack remembered he was supposed to go see the medical examiner this afternoon. So he headed off to his office. When Jack got to the medical examiner's office, he asked the M.E. what information he had for the detective. He told Jack the DNA from the trunk of the car showed Allison was definitely held in it for some period of time since they found hair there belonging to Allison. Then he said they also found strands of the same duct tape in the trunk as used on Allison's hands and mouth.

Jack told the M.E. he could have told him all of that over the phone.

Then the M.E. told Jack, "We also found fingerprints in the trunk that weren't Allison's."

Jack asked, "So there were two people in the trunk?"

The M.E. just said all he could say was there had been another person in the trunk at some time as there were hair samples from a second person.

Jack asked, "Couldn't the fingerprints just be a result of someone putting something in the trunk?"

"The fingerprints are a result of someone lying on their back and touching the trunk lid." Jack started to frown and asked the M.E. if it were possible that this person got locked in the trunk accidentally.

The M.E. said, "There were also marks inside the trunk showing there was a struggle, and someone was kicking the trunk from the inside. Since Allison's legs were bound, it make sense this was someone other than Allison."

Jack was thinking what is going on here. The M.E. told Jack he could match the shoes to the marks on the trunk if Jack is able to bring them to him, and the same for the hair samples from the second person. He would need a hair sample to compare with the sample they have. Jack thanked the M.E. for all of the great information and left the office. As Jack drove back to his office, he kept thinking that the more they learn, the weirder this case becomes.

On the way back to his office, Jack received a call from one of his investigators telling him that John wanted to speak to him regarding these charges. Jack asked what it was about, and the investigator just stated he would only speak to Jack. Jack told the investigator he would be there in about five minutes.

When Jack arrived back at the station, he got the investigator to bring John into an interrogation room. Once John entered the room, Jack asked him what it was he had to say. John told Jack he wanted a deal with the district attorney's office, and he wanted protection from the people he could point a finger at. Jack asked what he was even talking about. John then said he knew these people who were doing robberies not just in this area but in other parts of the state. Jack asked why he would need protection from something that seemed to be pretty straightforward.

John then said, "These guys do strong arm robberies, wherein the suspects use deadly force to steal from another party. They have stolen high-priced jewelry, drugs from other drug dealers, money, and high-priced art."

"How could you be sure this information was on point?"

"If my information doesn't check out, then you owe me nothing. But if it does, I get a deal and protection."

Jack told John to sit tight while he makes a call to the district attorney.

Jack went into his office to call the district attorney's office and tell them what John had just told him. The DA's office told Jack they would come down to interview John and then decide what kind of deal they would be willing to do with him. Jack got off the phone and went back into the room where John was. He told John that the DA's office would send someone down to interview him before they would commit to anything, but it would be tomorrow since it's so late. Jack then left John in the room waiting for them to come for his interview. One member of Jack's team took John to a cell in the Forsyth County jail to stay until tomorrow. Jack and his staff went home for the day.

On Tuesday, October 15, Jack awakened really positive, hoping the lab results from the postmortem viability test performed on Allison's fetus will show the father's DNA. The only way that would help locate the father was of course the DNA would have to be in the system. Also, during the night, Jack got a message saying the district attorney's office was issuing the material witness warrant for Heather. Jack was excited too to see what information John had and how that too might impact this case. All in all, Jack was hoping this day would be insightful for the investigation and hopefully help the team solve this mystery.

When Jack arrived at the office about 9:00 a.m., he was hoping the lab may have already called, but the other investigators advised Jack there was no news as yet. The investigator who was there told Jack that two policemen had gone to pick up Heather, and John had been transported from the jail back to the interrogation room. Jack was very glad to finally hear Heather was going to have to answer for her part, if any, in the murder of Allison. Jack had just gone into his office to get his other messages when one of the assistant district attorney's showed up to interview John. The ADA asked Jack to join her in the interview room.

Jack and the ADA went into the interrogation room where John was waiting. Upon entering the room and introducing the ADA to John, she asked John what information he had that he felt was worth them making a deal with him. John began by asking them to tape the interview so he would have a record of the conversation and any deals she put on the table. The ADA looked at Jack, and they both agreed with John's request. Jack went into his office to obtain a recorder and came back for the interview.

When Jack came back into the room, he handed the ADA the recorder, and she began by turning on the recorder and then stating who was in the room and she was there at the request of John Gordon to hear information regarding his illegal activity, his interaction with other criminals, and his willingness to work as an informant for the police department in exchange for some type of deal to get his current charges reduced or dropped. She also stated for the record that Detective Jack Williams was also in the room as not only a witness but as the detective on record and the arresting detective for John Gordon.

She asked John to state his full legal name as well as his other aliases. John stated his legal name was Rodney Jones, no middle name, and his aliases were Jimmy Little and now John Gordon. She asked John why he used other names, and John stated he had some legal issues over the years and found the need for other names in order to obtain employment as well as to hide from people who wanted to know his whereabouts for a variety of reasons.

The ADA then asked John, "Was everything recorded thus far accurate and true to the best of his knowledge?"

John answered, "Yes."

The ADA then asked John if he wanted an attorney present, and John stated he did not. The ADA asked Jack to read John his rights and asked John if he understood these rights, and John responded he did but asked why she was reading him his rights. He thought this was just a conversation, and he was not being charged for anything he would say to her or Jack.

She said to John, "You were arrested for a robbery, correct?"

John stated that was correct.

She stated she wanted to make sure he knew this conversation, as he called it, was outside the charge of robbery unless he could convince her he was not the person who ordered the robbery, and he would give up that person as well as testify against them in court. John agreed. The ADA then stated for the record that any admissions by John during this interview would not result in him being charged unless it was a crime he acted in alone with no direction by another person. She asked John if that was satisfactory. He answered yes.

The ADA asked, "What crimes had he committed to get his criminal record?"

John stated she must have the records in her file.

She said, "I need you to tell me what you were arrested for."

John told her he had stolen a bicycle when he was sixteen and got caught. And then when he was nineteen, he was caught with stolen goods.

The ADA asked what that had to do with anyone else?"

John said the goods that were in his possession belonged to someone else.

"Who was this person? You have to tell me everything or we have no deal."

John stated they belonged to a man who worked for Tony Bolero.

She asked for the man's name, and John said, "All I know was the man's first name, Fred."

Jack asked if he could question John and she stated he could.

Jack asked him if he knew where this Fred was, and John said he didn't know where he lived, but he knew Fred had come into the restaurant.

"Was Fred trying to get you to commit a crime?"

John stated no. "He came in to see Allison."

Jack looked like he had been punched in the stomach after he heard that. He asked if John heard any of the conversation the two of them had.

John said, "I know it was about her videos and photos on the Internet. I also know he gave her some very expensive diamond earrings."

Jack asked if John could identify them. John described what he had seen Allison wearing, and Jack remembered the description was an exact match for the earrings he had seen on Allison also. Jack then asked John if he knew where the earrings were now.

"I do not know where the earrings are," John stated. "Fred came back into the restaurant one night and he and Allison had an argument over something, and she told him to leave."

Jack asked what happened then.

John stated Allison was crying, and he heard her call her mom and tell her she wanted to sit down with her after she got off work to tell her everything. Jack then asked John if Allison was wearing the earrings the night she disappeared. John stated the last time he saw her wearing them was before she left for home.

John asked if she was wearing them when they found her, and Jack stated she was not. Jack asked John, "Did you see anyone in the parking lot when Allison got off work that evening?"

"Right before she got off work, there had been a car that drove through the lot but left."

"Why did you notice the car?"

"The car came in with the headlights shining in the front window of the restaurant."

Jack asked if he could describe the car, and John stated no. "The headlights were too bright."

"Did you happen to see a license number?"

"John stated he never saw the back of the car well enough to read the number."

Jack asked John why he had not come forth before now, and John said he couldn't afford to get caught up in that and have someone find out his real name. John went on to say that when he saw Fred in the restaurant the first time, he knew Allison was in big trouble. John said, "This bitch had no idea who she was messing with."

The ADA spoke up, "So Fred knew you and Allison?"

"Yes."

"How do we know he wasn't there after you since you had property belonging to Fred when you got arrested before?"

John answered, "Because when I started doing robberies for Fred and Tony, my slate was wiped clean. That was our deal."

She then asked John if he had ever gotten his instructions for the robberies directly from Tony Bolero.

"Tony is a smart guy, and he uses other people to do his dirty work. But Fred had told me this was for Tony."

She asked John what robberies were done that either he was a part of or knew about.

John went into great detail regarding the robberies he was involved in naming places, times, items taken, and the other robbers. Both Jack and the ADA knew of each robbery he described and knew he was being truthful. She asked John if he could tell Jack where the other robbers were, and John told her he could but only if they had a deal on his charges. The ADA agreed to drop his charges if his information was accurate and resulted in the other robbers being found and arrested. John agreed.

Jack asked John if he knew Allison was pregnant, and John stated he had no idea until he read it in the newspaper and saw it on the television. John spent the next hour giving details as to the robber's names and where to find them. He also told where the stolen items were and which ones were sold to pawnshops or other persons who buy stolen goods. In all, the group had committed over twelve robberies and had stolen some $200,000 worth of various items.

The ADA then asked John if he knew of anyone who might have been murdered during the time he has known

Fred or Tony. John stated there was a man who once owed some money to Tony and him, and one of the other robbers was taken as muscle to scare this guy. John then said that the guy pulled a gun on Fred, and he shot the man four times in the chest. She asked where this occurred, and John gave them the details. Then she asked what happened next, and John stated they were told to duct tape his hands and feet and then wrap the man's body in plastic before dumping him in a dry well out in the country.

She asked if he could remember where the body was dumped. John stated he could take them to it. She asked John if he knew the name of this man, and he stated he never heard the man's name nor had he heard Fred mention it. John then said he was scared to death after that, and that was when he changed his name to his deceased uncle's name, John Gordon. She asked if he still worked for Fred or Tony.

John stated, "You don't say no when Tony tells you to do something or you won't be around very long. Tony will kill you just to have something to do."

Jack asked John if he knew if Tony and Fred ran this video ring.

"There was a couple of other guys as far as I knew, but I never met either one of them."

Jack asked if there was any way he could find out the guys who run that part of the business.

"Do I have to?"

Jack said, "We need your help. You can get a lot more information than we can."

John stated he would try. Jack then asked John if he happened to have any of this duct tape they used when this other guy got killed. John stated he did not have any, but he might be able to get some from Fred. "He had a couple of rolls in his vehicle."

Jack asked what kind of vehicle it was, and John kind of shrugged his shoulders and said he was so scared he really didn't notice the kind of car.

Jack excused himself for a minute from the interview and then, called the medical examiner, and asked if he could match the duct tape used on Allison if he brought him a roll of the tape. The M.E. responded it was a very common type of tape, and the best he could do was probably match it to when the batch was run, and perhaps the number of rolls produced during that run, and possibly who the rolls might have gone to.

Jack said, "That's a lot of maybes."

The M.E. stated that there could have been thousands of rolls produced on that run and shipped all over the country. He wouldn't know that until the batch had been identified. He went on to say the tape was in the fluids in the dumpster. Jack thanked him for trying anyway and went back to the interview room.

When Jack got back into the room, the ADA was asking John about other enterprises Fred and Tony might be involved in. John told her he knew Fred had mentioned prostitution in the past as well as loan sharking. She asked John if he had any proof of these other activities.

John said, "I can show you where some of the people work who owed them money. I know of a couple of places where they might be running the prostitution."

She asked John to show Jack where these might be, and he agreed.

John asked both Jack and the ADA if they were going to give him protection, and the ADA agreed she would speak to the FBI when all of this was over to make sure John was safe. John at least felt better for the moment.

It was well after 1:00 p.m. when Jack and the ADA decided to break for lunch so they could discuss what they had heard from John. They agreed to come back to meet John about 2:00 p.m., but in the meantime, John would have to stay at the office where they would supply him with his lunch. Jack and the ADA went to a nearby grill so they could sit down in a corner and have a private conversation regarding all the things John had stated. Jack asked her if she was going to be the one to process the paperwork for John, and she responded by saying, "I'll prepare the paperwork after we have a couple of these people in jail or catch them red-handed with the evidence."

Jack told the ADA that John is under the impression she would prepare the papers for dismissal against him in exchange for his cooperation. She told Jack she does not usually dismiss any charges without getting something up front. Jack stated the fact that he was willing to take them to these people and the crime scenes should prove his part of the bargain. After their lunch, Jack finally just told the ADA that he was not comfortable with this bait and switch tactic, and he wanted no part of it. The ADA then said she will prepare the paperwork this afternoon for John to sign, and they returned to Jack's office.

They got back to the office and met with John so they could go over the details and the time frame so they along with the team can get together and start following through gaining the items sold that were stolen, as well as arresting those involved in these robberies. The lady ADA told John that she will have the papers ready for him to sign later this afternoon, saying the state will take a dismissal of the charges levied against him. Jack told John he needed to stay at Jack's office until the papers are signed as Jack has other things he has to follow up on this afternoon. John agreed.

Jack got an e-mail from the postmortem viability test lab, stating the results were in from Allison Tuttle's sample and that there was a determination that resulted from the sample; however, the DNA was not on file in any law enforcement databases both statewide and federal. Jack thought to himself this was the news he expected but not what he had hoped for.

Jack copied his other investigators and was also notified that Heather had been brought in using handcuffs since she and her mother caused a disturbance at the home for fighting with police during the arrest. The mother was detained until Heather could be put in handcuffs, and then the mom was released. Jack was looking forward to interviewing Heather.

Jack came out of his office and asked which interview room Heather was in. When Jack walked in, Heather was very angry and told Jack that her mother told her not to say anything until her attorney got here. Jack stepped out of the room and told another investigator to let him know when the attorney arrives.

In the meantime, Jack went back to his office to prepare a list of potential fathers of Allison's baby, whom they would need to get a DNA sample from to rule out as not only a potential father but perhaps a murderer. Jack started thinking about all of the potential fathers just thus far. Just in a few minutes, Jack thought of more than 130 men who would have to be tested. Jack thought they would begin by testing the most obvious ones and then expand their net, if necessary. The DA's office called Jack, and the lady ADA stated she had the papers ready and would come by to have John sign them. Jack agreed. By the time Jack had finished his list, the attorney for Heather had arrived, so Jack went back into the interview room.

As Jack entered the interview room, Heather started mouthing off, and her attorney told her not to speak unless she was answering a question. The attorney introduced himself to Jack and wanted to say from the onset he thought this was misconduct by the police and the district attorney's office, and he had all intentions of filing a civil suit against the state, the county, the department, and Jack personally.

Jack replied to the attorney, "If she had just answered the questions initially, she could have been excluded, and we wouldn't even be having this conversation."

The attorney told Jack she would only answer questions he approved, and Jack told the attorney she would answer all of his questions or be held in contempt and sent to jail until she cooperated.

The attorney then stated, "Then I just won't allow her to answer any questions."

"Good counselor, then we will arrest you for hindering prosecution and hold you in jail too."

The attorney told Jack he could ask her anything.

Heather spoke up, "I'm not answering any questions."

The attorney told Heather she would answer questions, or she would be held in jail forever unless she told the police what they wanted to know. Heather said, "It's not fair." The attorney told her it seldom is.

Jack started by asking Heather why she did not want to answer questions that might help the police find Allison's killer.

Heather stated she didn't want to get involved since Allison was doing things she didn't agree with.

Jack asked, "What kinds of things?"

She told Jack she should have spoken up a long time ago when Allison was going through this phase of making one bad decision after another.

Jack asked Heather if she could just start at the beginning. "Heather, I know you and Allison have had your ups and downs, but she needs your help. And the baby she was carrying needs your help also."

Heather said she was not shocked to find out Allison was pregnant. She knew Allison was in way over her head, but she was the only one who could not see that.

Jack then asked Heather if she had any idea who could do such a thing.

She said, "I know of a few people if you want to know the truth."

"Who?"

"There was a guy who came to their school and was waiting for her when Allison got out one day."

Jack said, "I think I'm lost. Can we just start from when you think she got in over her head?"

Heather stated she would. She started telling Jack it had been a few months ago, and Allison came to school wearing clothing shorter than she normally wore. She noticed Allison was wearing better clothes than she had worn since she had known her.

Jack asked if Allison ever mentioned where these clothes were coming from.

Heather said she assumed at first that the job at the restaurant must be paying really well, or she was getting great tips. She said she was at the restaurant one day after that and asked the other waitresses if they too were making good money. The other waitresses told Heather they weren't getting rich, and the tips sucked. Heather admitted when she heard that, she began to question where Allison was getting this money. She also remembered Allison wearing more jewelry than she had ever worn.

Jack asked Heather if she ever just asked Allison if someone was buying her jewelry. She stated Allison came back with, "Are you jealous. I deserve pretty things."

Heather told Jack that when she and Allison tried to bond, it always seemed to start an argument, and usually the argument always began around Allison's beauty and her worth, mostly to herself. Allison would make comments about how other people appreciated her beauty and why Heather couldn't. I would say things like "I don't need to comment on your beauty. You do that enough on your own." Allison would then become angry since Heather was running her down, at least in Allison's eyes. Jack was starting to get the real picture between the two young women. Jack asked Heather to please go on with her story.

She told Jack that the next thing she noticed was Allison acting so prissy in front of the football team and the guys at school. She said Allison would go out of her way to shake her ass in front of any male. Jack immediately started thinking this was almost word-for-word the way John described Allison. He wondered why they would choose the same language. Then Heather went on by saying that Allison started wearing all these new shoes and fancy makeup. She said there was no way she was making money at the restaurant for these things.

Jack said, "By the way, when I first saw Allison at the restaurant, I noticed she was wearing some very expensive diamond earrings. Do you happen to know where she got them?"

Heather stated she had seen them but had no idea where she got them, but probably some guy. Jack knew what Jennifer had told him and knew Heather was lying to one of them. Allison always ragged on her parents for not buying her what she wanted so Allison figured out a way to get what she wanted. Heather said that Allison would do anything to be popular, and she told Heather she had put some of her pictures on the Internet. Heather said this video had been made of her and that was on the Internet too. She said she warned Allison. "This was going too fast, but Allison just laughed and said 'I can handle myself.' All Allison talked about was making money, and showing off her body on the Internet. To make things worse, Allison met this guy at school like I told you earlier, and I was scared for her, but she seemed to know this guy. When Allison drove off, he drove off right behind her. Allison wound up going to this place he had talked her into to make another video that would give her thousands of people watching her and paying to do it."

Jack asked if Heather knew where they went to make this video, but she said Allison never told her. Heather then said, "The video got posted, but only after this guy had drugged her while she made this crap." Heather elaborated that Allison sent her a password to get into the video, and she was so ashamed to even see it with Allison doing things that she normally wouldn't do. She explained that Allison was excited about the number of people who watched it and the money she made so she could do anything and buy anything she wanted.

Jack remarked, "So it was all about the money."

Heather agreed. Then she told Jack that some of the people from the video started showing up at the restaurant, which made Allison nervous and excited at the same time. In Allison's eyes, she was famous or some movie star or something. She talked about this one guy, named Fred, who came into the restaurant and really scared Allison.

Jack asked, "How did you know?"

She answered, "Allison used to e-mail or text all this stuff to me every day. I felt bad, like it was my fault Allison died."

"How?" Jack asked.

"I was the one who told Allison she should threaten this guy who posted it and tell him she would go to the police if he didn't take down the site." Heather said that the guy told Allison not to get stupid because stupid people wind up dead. She started crying, saying she didn't mean to get Allison killed; she was just trying to get her to wake up and get out of this mess.

Jack asked her why she didn't tell Allison to call him.

She said, "You have no idea of how many times I begged her to call you, but she was ashamed and didn't want her family to find out and be embarrassed about this whole situation." Heather said she asked Allison what she was going to do the day she went missing, and Allison just said she had not made up her mind. She told Jack he had no idea of the nights she cried herself to sleep, worried about Allison.

Jack asked if Chuck or John ever came on to Allison, and she stated that both of them were perverts, and she had to fight them off from all their groping and feeling her up. She said, "Truth be known, I think she actually got excited for them to touch her as much as she hated them touching her, if that made sense."

Jack said, "It was the thrill of the moment."

Heather agreed.

Jack asked Heather if Allison had ever given her anything to keep for her.

She replied she kept some clothing from time to time when Allison asked her to.

He asked, "Was there anything at her house now?"

"I might have a few things."

Jack asked if she ever kept jewelry for Allison there all the time, knowing she did keep some once in a while.

Heather stuttered and said, "I don't think so."

Jack couldn't help but wonder if she was keeping the jewelry for herself or if she sold it, so he asked if she would mind letting him look to see Allison's things that she had.

Heather said she would have to ask her mom.

"It might really help to find Allison's killer if you would let me look at the clothing you had at the house."

Then Heather's attorney spoke up and said he would need a warrant.

Jack just shook his head and stated, "If that's what it takes, but we also want to see her computer and all of her e-mails."

Heather said, "That stuff is personal, and I don't want anyone looking at my computer."

"Heather, if you don't voluntarily let us look, we will get a warrant to seize these items."

The attorney asked on what grounds.

Jack replied, "On the grounds she just admitted to having items belonging to Allison, and we believe her to possibly be in possession of stolen property."

"She did not steal anything."

"We have information from another source who says Heather kept jewelry at her house, which we know now some of which was stolen in robberies and is evidence of these robberies. If she doesn't turn these items over, then she will be arrested as an accomplice in these robberies and for being in possession of stolen property."

The attorney whispered to Heather and then stated that Jack and the team could look through her belongings as long as she was not charged with any crime.

Jack said, "If she cooperates in this investigation, and she had no part in the robberies or the murder, he would agree to that."

The attorney stated he wanted to be present at the time of this search and seizure, and Jack agreed.

Jack then said, "Heather was not allowed to phone her mother or anyone else until the search had been conducted so she couldn't get someone else to remove the items."

The attorney agreed.

Jack told Heather, "We found your fingerprints on Allison's car. Do you know why that may be?"

Heather stated they were friends, so she had been in the car.

"I understand that part, but the part I don't understand is why your prints were in the system?"

"I don't understand."

Heather's attorney spoke up and told Heather that for them to be in the system, she had been fingerprinted at some point in time, meaning she'd been in trouble with the law before. The attorney said, "These records were sealed since she is a juvenile."

Jack said, "We are not looking for some petty larceny case, counselor. We are looking for her friend's murderer."

The attorney answered, "She was picked up for petty larceny. She took a pack of cigarettes without paying for them."

"Okay," Jack stated.

Jack left the room to get some other investigators prepared as they are going to Heather's house right away and bringing the forensic team. Jack asked where John was when he noticed the interview room was empty. One of Jack's team told him the ADA had gotten him to sign the papers, and she received a call and stated she had to go and that she was finished with John, so they released him.

Jack said, "Oh no, he was not supposed to be released. He was going to show me where a body was buried. Oh my God, what a mistake to let him go. Get that ADA on the phone to see why she let him go." Jack went back in and told Heather they were ready to go to her house now.

One of the investigators brought a van around for the attorney and Heather to travel in with two investigators. Jack followed behind the van until they got to her house as agreed. Heather and her attorney went in the house first to tell her mom they were there to look around and for Heather's computer. Heather's mom was angry, but Heather told her it was either that or she would have to stay in jail.

Jack and the investigators started searching the house by looking into Heather's room for any signs of Allison's clothes or jewelry. One of the forensic team got on Heather's computer and called Jack over to inform him that some of the files had been erased, but not from the hard drive. The forensic investigator told Jack they needed to take the computer with them, and he agreed. While Jack was working with this investigator, another one came over and told him they found something in a metal box in the attic of the home. Jack went in the attic to see several pieces of jewelry and some clothing too small for Heather. They brought the things downstairs and asked Heather if she recognized these items. Heather stated she had no idea who put the things in the attic, and Jack reminded her that they had fingerprinted her, and she better tell him the truth. She finally admitted she hid those things up there so her mom wouldn't find them. Jack then told Heather they were taking her computer with them. He also told her that they had called the cell phone company and got a copy of her bill and a map of her recent locations. Jack recalled that Heather had a look on her face like she just got busted with dope in her pocketbook.

Heather asked when she would get her computer back.

Jack just said. "When we're done, I'll call you."

All of the team left and went back to their office.

Jack got a call from ADA, telling him she thought John was ready to be released. Jack told the her he needed to get with John about the body and the stolen jewelry and the other robbers. She apologized and stated she got a call from her boss, and she forgot. When Jack arrived back at his office, there was a message on his phone from one of the units who checked out pawnshops for stolen items. The message stated the name of a pawnshop that had searched their inventory for the jewelry Jack had described, and they believed they had found the diamond earrings Jack was looking for. He was very excited to see who pawned them. Jack and the team went home for the day.

On Wednesday, October 16, when Jack woke up, all he could think about was finding out who pawned these earrings. Jack was on his way to his office when he got a call from John saying he was going to meet with the guy he had told Jack about.

Jack asked, "Which guy?"

John stated, "The one I told you about who had disposed of the body."

"Why are you meeting with that guy?"

"I am going to try to get some of the duct tape from his car if he could."

Jack told him to be careful and let him know when he had possession of the tape. He told John not to forget that they needed to go to the place John had told him about where the body was dumped.

John told Jack he would get with him on that when he brought back the duct tape.

Jack called the pawnshop and went by there on his way to his office. When he got there, he met with the owner and looked at the photographs of the earrings they had taken in pawn. When Jack looked at the pictures, he knew right away these were the earrings he saw on Allison the first day he saw her at the restaurant. Then he asked to see the pawn ticket. When he saw the ticket, he was blown away at who pawned the jewelry, John Gordon. Jack thought that if John pawned the earrings, then he was the last person to see Allison alive that night, especially when John testified he saw Allison wearing them when she left the restaurant. As much as Jack wanted to have John picked up right away, he didn't dare call him for fear he may already be with the man he knows is a murderer. Jack decided it would be better to wait until John called him and convince him to come to his office. Jack got a copy of the pawn slip and called his office to let them know he was on his way and to issue an APB, all points bulletin, for John Gordon and his aliases.

Jack arrived at his office where the forensic guys told him they had identified a lot of the e-mails and deleted files on Heather's computer. He asked if there was something specific that showed anything new on Allison's murder. The forensic guy told Jack they found e-mails showing Heather knew more than she was telling, and he needed to come see the information for himself. Jack started looking at the files, deleted from the computer but not the hard drive, when he saw a file marked John. The investigator opened the file for Jack, and he started seeing communications where John and Heather were both trashing Allison and talking about her and the people she was hanging around.

Jack was not surprised when he saw the same thing on both. The two had commented on how trashy Allison was and how she liked to show it off to any men. Another e-mail was between Heather and some of their other school friends, who commented on where Allison was getting all her money. One of the girls remarked she was a whore and selling it to anyone with a dime. The investigator then showed Jack a few files with photographs that had been removed but not erased, which showed Allison with several men, some of whom Jack knew and some not known.

The investigators had printed some photos for Jack of different men Allison had shared with Heather and were on her computer also. Jack was no longer shocked to see Allison in compromising positions with numerous men. The investigators then showed Jack the one thing he was not expecting: an e-mail Allison had forwarded to Heather, showing there were more than four hundred men who had signed up to see Allison naked and doing sex acts. Jack wished they had a list of these people and not just an e-mail showing the number. He just sat and shook his head, thinking he had a feeling this was going to be bad, but not this bad. The team told him they were still getting things off the computer and would keep him informed. Jack asked if they ever got any fingerprints of the photos left on Jack's doorstep, but they stated the envelope and the photos were wiped clean.

An All-American Girl

About 11:00 a.m. on Wednesday, Jack started thinking about the list he had made with the possible suspects for Allison's baby. He called the forensic team and asked one of them to meet him at the restaurant. Jack met the forensic technician at the restaurant and went in to see Chuck. When Jack and the technician came in, Chuck asked, "What the heck could you possibly want now?"

Jack told Chuck that the DNA they got from the baby was not in the system, and he wanted him to give up a sample so he could be ruled out.

Chuck said, "You're out of your mind."

"If you don't have anything to hide, then why wouldn't you want to be eliminated?"

"I'll do it if that will keep you out of here."

"It won't take but a couple of seconds."

The technician then took a swab and a sample of Chuck's saliva to be analyzed and left the building.

Jack then decided to get a comparative sample from Allison's dad and be able to eliminate him at the same time. Jack asked the technician to follow him to the Tuttle home. When the two of them arrived at the Tuttle's house, they rang the bell, and Paul answered the door. Paul looked confused, so Jack explained they needed a comparison DNA from a male family member to match against the suspects when they are tested. Paul agreed, and the technician took the same sample from him. Paul asked if they were getting any closer, and Jack advised they are making headway and hope to have the killer in custody soon. The technician and Jack left the Tuttle's house.

Next stop for the DNA test was to the school and getting samples from each member of the football team and Michael, the ex-boyfriend. When the two arrived at the school, they advised the principal of what they were doing. The principal was worried about the young men's rights and their privacy, so Jack called the ADA to get a court order to force the underage kids to give up their DNA. The ADA got a judge to sign off and brought the court order to the school.

Getting the DNA from the large number of young men took a couple of hours.

The technician went back to the office to begin the DNA analysis, and Jack started thinking that he should have heard from John by now. Jack too went back to his office to wait for John to call and see where the DNA samples led the case.

Jack noticed it was well after 3:00 p.m. and still no word from John. The first thing Jack thought was John had fled the jurisdiction, knowing they were going to find out he might have killed Allison. The lady DA called Jack to see if he had heard from John.

Jack said, "I heard from him earlier today, but I had also learned he was the one who pawned the diamond earrings.

John was meeting with Fred to see if he could also get a sample of the duct tape."

The ADA said, "So John was just telling us what we wanted to hear to get released."

"I'm afraid John was also the one who killed Allison."

She again apologized to Jack for letting him go.

Jack said, "I have an APB out for John at this time. Hopefully, some law enforcement person will see him and pick him up."

She thanked Jack for understanding about her releasing him and asked him to keep her posted.

Once Jack was off the phone, another thought crossed his mind: what if John went to go see Fred, and he somehow knew that John had been talking to the police, and Fred either killed him or had him killed?

About 5:00 p.m., the M.E.'s office interrupted Jack by telling him they had some of the results from the DNA Buccal tests performed earlier today. So Jack left his office to go into the forensic office. One of the team told Jack all members of the football team checked thus far were not a match for the DNA from the fetus. The M.E. then told Jack that Chuck was not a match for the DNA either. Jack couldn't help but think the match was going to be with either John or someone with the video people who filmed Allison. Jack had come to face the fact that John was not going to be coming back either way.

Jack just sat in his office, wondering if he had missed something. He was replaying the events since September 24, when Allison's body was found. Jack was also looking at the dry erasable boards where all of the clues and notes were written down. As he replayed those events and remembering the interviews with the key people in this case, he noticed a note about a girl written in an e-mail they recovered on Allison's computer, where she was threatening Allison about the earrings. Jack wondered what she meant by that and exactly whose earrings these actually were. He thought that if he could find the author of that e-mail, it may open some doors for him to find the killer. He kept thinking Heather lied about the earrings, and the classmate also lied about the same earrings. But why? Where did these earrings come from, and why were they so important? Who had them before? How did Allison get them, and from whom? Jack knew he had to get to the bottom of that part of this puzzle. Jack couldn't help but think if he found out who owned these earrings, he would also find people associated with this video ring. He went home for the day since it was already 7:00 p.m. and he was hungry.

On Thursday, October 17, Jack was having breakfast at home when he thought back to something John had said during his interview. John said that when he was nineteen, he was arrested for possession of stolen goods. And when Jack asked if he stole the goods, he said he was holding them for someone else. Jack immediately called the DA's office to get the information about the case. The DA told Jack they would get the information and get back to him. Before the DA hung up, Jack also asked if they had an address for John's uncle who passed away and if they would give Jack that as well. He finished up what he was doing and headed off to his office.

When Jack arrived at his office, he received a phone call from the district attorney's office with the information he had asked for. Jack was told John Gordon was using one of his other aliases when he was nineteen and arrested for possession of stolen property in South Carolina. The investigator's at the time tracked the stolen property back to a well-known criminal, William Thacker, who had been arrested dozens of times for robbery, soliciting prostitution, bribery, possession of stolen property, and other crimes. The DA told Jack that Thacker was last known to be in the Georgia, South Carolina, area. Jack thanked the DA and then started thinking South Carolina is not that far from Charlotte, NC, where Allison's car was found.

Jack thought that since John pawned the earrings, which he could have easily gotten off Allison, perhaps he was working with this Thacker character. Jack was also thinking this Thacker guy could be one of the guys who came into the restaurant that no one seemed to know. Jack called back to the DA's office to see if they had a photo of this William Thacker. The district attorney's office sent one over, and Jack was going to take it to the restaurant to see if anyone there recognized the man in the photo. Jack took the photo of Thacker and put it in a six-pack so the viewer would have to examine each one to see if they recognized anyone they've seen before at or around the restaurant.

Jack left his office and went out to the restaurant with the photo array. When he got to the restaurant, he walked in. Chuck had already seen him get out of the car. Chuck said, "Please tell me you're here to eat."

Jack asked Chuck if he would look at the photos and see if he saw anyone he recognized.

Chuck looked at the photos and then said, "No, should I?"

Jack stated he believed one of these men has been in the restaurant recently.

Chuck glanced again at the photos and then said, "I've never seen any of these guys."

"Is it okay for me to show these to your waitresses and any regular customers?" Jack asked.

Chuck reluctantly agreed.

When Jack showed the photos to the other waitresses, they immediately pointed at the photo of William Thacker. One of the waitresses even said, "I remember he came in and wanted to see John. Don't you remember, Chuck, he even spoke to you?"

Chuck said, "I didn't remember talking to the man."

Then Jack showed the photos to a few regular customers, and two of them remembered seeing this guy in the restaurant. One customer said, "He came in when Allison was here, and she said something to him and another guy about some photos on the Internet."

Jack asked the customers if they remembered when that was, and they thought a minute and then said either the night she disappeared or one or two nights just before that.

Jack wrote down their names, addresses, and phone numbers in case they would have to testify as to what they saw and heard. Jack thanked them for their cooperation and told Chuck they needed to talk.

Jack and Chuck walked back into his office. Jack asked Chuck how he knew this guy. Chuck said he didn't remember talking to this person.

Jack commented, "You want to be very careful here, Chuck. If you lie to me again, you will be going to jail."

"I want my attorney," Chuck said.

Jack told him he could call his attorney from the station, and he read Chuck his rights and took him off to his office to meet his attorney for hindering prosecution and lying to a police officer. The entire restaurant was shocked to see

Jack bring Chuck out of the office in handcuffs. Jack called his office to let them know he was coming in with Chuck.

On the way back, Chuck advised Jack that he wanted to call his attorney as soon as they arrived, and he was making no statement until he spoke to the attorney. Once they arrived, Chuck made his phone call and was placed in a holding cell. By the time Jack got back to his office, several things had happened. The forensic team had left a note for Jack to come by. So that was Jack's first stop.

Jack went over to the forensic lab and asked what was going on. He was told the forensic guys had found out some of the information from Heather's computer. Jack asked if they were going to keep him in suspense. The lab tech stated they had found files on Heather's computer marked personal, and in the file there was a password, in fact numerous passwords, to see the videos Allison had starred in. Jack asked what was so great about that. He said they already knew that Heather had seen the videos, which they knew were from Allison's e-mails.

But the lab tech went on to say, "But these had other people's e-mails attached since they were copied to Allison from another computer." The lab tech stated they knew John Gordon had seen the videos as well since his e-mail was on Heather's e-mail list. The tech also stated Chuck had seen these video's for the same reason.

Jack asked if there were any other e-mails in this link, and the tech said they found three more e-mails but were unsure of the owners as yet. He asked if there was anything else, and they stated that the fiberglass fibers that were on the duct tape Allison had around her hands was definitely the same kind of fiberglass used in furnace filters, some auto filters, and heating and cooling systems. The techs stated they were still working on trying to pinpoint the exact material and then they could narrow the search. Jack asked them if they ever got any information from Allison's cell phone and the tech said the phone was smashed and for some reason the chip in the phone was never found. Jack said, "So the phone was useless without the chip." The tech just nodded. Jack thanked them for the information and left to go back to his office since Chuck's attorney was there waiting to see his client.

When Jack got back to his office to interview Chuck, his attorney stated he wanted to have a private conversation with his client before he answered any questions. Jack gave them a few minutes alone and waited outside until the attorney was ready. After about twenty minutes, the attorney stated they were ready for the interview but that everything was off the record until they have an agreement.

Jack told them he would have to know what this was about.

The attorney asked Jack if he was familiar with the name Tony Bolero.

Jack asked, "What information does he have that will put him away. How could Chuck become involved with people like Tony Bolero?"

The attorney told Chuck to tell Jack what he wanted to know.

Chuck stated that the restaurant was not doing well, and there was a guy who came in one day and told him he could help with his money problems. Chuck asked how, and the guy said if he was willing to let him leave items there for another person to pick up later, he would pay him for his trouble. Chuck asked what kinds of things, and the man stated he really didn't need to know and it made no difference anyway. Chuck asked what kind of money, and the man told him they would start leaving small packages, and as he became more trustworthy, they would increase the volume. Again, Chuck questioned what kind of money. The man stated to start with $1,000 a week and would go up as far as he was willing to go with the venture. Chuck was going to close the restaurant if he didn't find a way to get some money coming in. So he agreed.

Jack asked if the man he spoke to was Tony Bolero.

Chuck looked at the attorney and said, "No, but it was someone working for Tony as I found out later."

"Who was it?" Jack asked.

The attorney stated, "That's all you get until we have a deal." The attorney stated that Chuck could give them Tony Bolero, Fred, and some other criminals. Chuck added that he knew they were going to kill John anyway.

Jack asked how he knew, and Chuck said he was told John was working for the police.

"How do we know you did not tell these people?"

The attorney told Jack that his client was not going to say another word until they had a deal of immunity.

Jack told the attorney, "That is up to the DA's office. I need to make a few phone calls regarding any agreement." Jack made some calls but was finally told they would have to deal with the US attorney's office since Tony Bolero was a big-time criminal and was linked to the mob. Since it was late in the day, Jack was told that the US attorney's office would send someone down to speak to Chuck in the morning.

Jack went back to Chuck's attorney and told him there was nothing they could do until the morning.

By now it was almost 7:00 p.m., so Jack had Chuck moved to a cell in the Forsyth County jail.

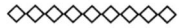

Jack got a call from the medical examiner's office regarding the other DNA tests, and when he called the medical examiner back, he was told that all of the football team was cleared, and they had done the Buccal panel from Paul and matched it to the DNA from Allison and the fetus. The medical examiner stated Paul's DNA was similar to Allison's of course since he was her father, and then went on to say the fetus's DNA was very close to Paul's, which means the father had to be from this same family. Jack asked what he was saying, and the examiner stated it has to be a family member of Allison's. Jack asked if was he sure, and the examiner said 100 percent sure.

Jack was stunned at the result. Was it Landon? Surely not. But based on that, it had to be him. Jack then told the examiner they would get the DNA sample from Landon. Jack called Paul and asked if he had a phone number for Landon, and Paul asked why. Jack just said he needed to speak to Landon immediately. Paul gave Jack the number, and Jack got off the phone to call Landon.

Jack apologized to Landon for calling so late in the evening. Jack explained to him the medical examiner had taken DNA samples from all members of the football team at Allison's school as well as from his dad and other men. Landon asked why would he have gotten this from their dad, and Jack explained it was to pattern the DNA so they could prove the paternity of the child in court. When they found the real dad of the fetus, there would be no way the father could deny this was his child.

Landon told Jack, "So I guess now you're going to tell me you want my DNA as well."

Jack stated they would very much appreciate it if he would give a swab of his saliva. He was shocked when Landon refused.

Landon said, "You can't find the killer, so now you're going to try and blame this on our family. Hell, no. I'm not helping you arrest myself or my dad." Landon slammed the phone down.

Jack immediately started thinking how odd of a reaction from someone who supposedly wanted to find the killer right away. He also thought perhaps he was just under so much stress that he overreacted. Jack was hoping during the night that Landon would think things over and see he was just trying to find the killer and the fetus's father so the family could get some closure. Jack finally went home for the day in hopes Landon would have a clearer view in the morning.

Friday morning, October 18, came, and Jack decided to eat out before going to his office. He went to a local diner and walked in only to find dozens of questions from the local residents about the Tuttle case. He told them he was not at liberty to discuss an open investigation but thanked them for taking an interest in the outcome. About the time Jack was getting ready to leave the diner, one of the patrons asked him what he was going to do about organized crime coming into this area. Jack asked the patron where he heard such a rumor. The patron stated he heard from the restaurant that some big criminal connected with the mob was working in the area with Chuck, the restaurant owner. Jack tried to tell the patron that there was no proof as to where this portion of the case was going. But nothing had been confirmed or denied regarding any involvement with the restaurant owner. Jack went on to say that gossip, while it is a normal response for people, does not bring clarity to the investigation but rather clouds the issues, making it difficult for law enforcement to do their job. Jack said, "I know I can count on all of you and your neighbors not to spread unsubstantiated rumors." He left the diner.

Jack stopped along the way and got fast food since his diner meal was diverted with having to answer all of the questions regarding the arrest of Chuck the restaurant owner and the whole mob-possibilities. When Jack got to his office, the team began by asking him if everything was all right since he was running late. Jack explained the incident at the diner and the rumors that were ramping up over Chuck's situation at the restaurant and then, to make it worse, someone had already mentioned to the gossip committee about the possibility of the mob coming to this small town. Jack explained that he defused the situation as best he could. One of Jack's team said, "It makes you wonder how these people get all this information and get it distributed in such a small amount of time." Another member of Jack's team told him the US attorney from the Eastern district in Greeneville, NC, should be here most any time.

Detective Jack called the medical examiner to let him know what happened when he called Landon. But he would continue to try and get the sample for comparison. Jack had Chuck transferred back from his jail cell to a holding cell. After Jack had taken care of some mundane issues in the office and was getting ready to go across town, the US attorney came into Jack's office.

After the introductions with Jack and his team, they sat down and brought the US attorney up to speed on the entire situation, encompassing the disappearance, the murder, and how they got to where they are today. Jack and his team also brought the attorney current on where Chuck, Tony Bolero, Fred, John, and others all fit into this puzzle. The attorney asked Jack what this guy Chuck was looking for, and Jack explained Chuck's attorney was looking for immunity on all charges. The US attorney told him he would listen to what this guy had to say, and then he and Jack would get back together and decide how important this information is to solving this girl's murder and to bring mobsters to bear and consequently to jail. The two men went in to see Chuck and his attorney.

Jack introduced the US attorney to Chuck and his attorney and then let the former take over the conversation. Chuck's attorney started by telling their side of the equation and how he wanted full immunity for anything Chuck may say during this interview. The US attorney stated he was not giving this guy immunity for anything until he heard what Chuck had to say. Chuck's attorney said that Chuck would give Jack information on unsolved cases that would take them years to solve, if they could ever solve them at all. The US attorney stated that depending on what Chuck had to say, and if he could connect these possible suspects to actual crimes, he would consider giving Chuck immunity. But only if he testified against these people in court and named all of the individuals in question so they could issue indictments. Chuck's attorney also asked for witness protection, and the US attorney agreed, but only after the suspects had been tried and sent to prison. The two attorneys agreed, and the interrogation began. Just like the agreement between John and the DA, the interrogation was recorded.

The US attorney said, "So let's see what you have to say."

Chuck started by stating his full name, address, and how he came to buy a restaurant in this area.

He was then asked. "Take us back to your past and when you first met any of these people you were going to name in criminal activity."

Chuck said, "As I told Detective Jack Williams, my restaurant was not thriving, and I was trying to find a way to make some extra money or get money coming into the restaurant. We had tried advertising, specials, coupons, and all of the normal ways to bring in cash, but nothing was working. One day, a man I had never met came into my restaurant and stated if I was willing to let them drop off some items or packages and have another individual pick them up later. I would get paid starting at $1,000 a week, and the more I let them drop off, the more money I would be getting."

The US attorney asked if Chuck was told what was in these packages.

He replied he was not. Chuck went on to say, "One of the packages was damaged when it was dropped off, and I could see it was jewelry, very nice jewelry, and diamond jewelry. I figured it was going to be drugs. But that package was jewelry, so I assumed the jewelry had been stolen or taken from a robbery."

The US attorney asked how Chuck got paid.

"Once a week, I would get a package with my money in it, along with the packages for the other person to pick up.

This went on for about a year. About two months ago, one of the packages was wet when I got it, and I tried to dry it off, and the paper came loose. It was a box with some type of medicine in it. It was a bottle of a sort of nasal spray, so I just wrapped it back up in some brown paper, and when the other guy came to pick up the packages, I told him I rewrapped it."

The US attorney asked if it had anything on the bottle.

"It had two letters and '141' marked on the label."

Jack asked the US attorney if they could take a break for a couple of minutes. And they stopped the recording.

Jack and the US attorney went into another room, and Jack explained the medical examiner's office had told him about this drug PT-141 that was running rampant in Europe, and this drug will be more powerful than ecstasy would ever be. But he had not heard of any in the United States as yet. Jack said that if they could catch the people who are bringing this into this country, this would be a huge catch. The US attorney told Jack to not say anything about that when they go back into the room. He added, "Let Chuck tell his story, then we will get him to keep taking deliveries until we find a delivery with these drugs in it. We can run this down and see where the drugs wind up."

The two men went back into the room where Chuck and his attorney were.

The US attorney apologized for the interruption and asked Chuck to continue telling them about the packages. He asked Chuck, "What was the largest number of packages you received weekly?"

Chuck answered, "I have had as many as sixty packages a week and gotten paid $4,000."

Chuck was asked where he stored that much inventory.

Chuck said, "I kept it in a locker, or if necessary, I kept it in a cooler or a storage chest in the cooler."

Jack asked if he knew where the diamond earrings Allison was wearing came from.

"The guy who brought me the packages gave them to her."

Jack asked how he knew this.

"The guy had taken a liking to Allison, and Allison came onto him when he was in the restaurant."

Jack asked the name of this guy.

"Kevin, that's the name he used with me, but I'm not sure if that was his real name."

Jack said, "We'll need you to look at the mug books to find this guy or sit down with a sketch artist."

Chuck agreed.

Jack asked how this guy was connected to Tony Bolero.

"One time when he was getting a delivery of packages, this other guy came in the restaurant and wanted me to know what a great job I had been doing in taking care of their product. He introduced himself to me as Tony Bolero. Not only that, Allison was also mesmerized by another guy who also had been coming in. I tried to warn Allison about this guy, but she just kept hanging all over him. He came into the restaurant to see John. His name was Fred. He and Allison had something going with these videos she was doing. 'I know,' she told one of the other waitresses, 'he worked for this big shot named Tony Bolero'." Chuck continued, "When John got pinched by you guys, I was asked by Kevin about his working with the cops. I told him that I knew nothing about it, but he said, 'Well when he surfaces let me know'. When John got out, he came here to pick up his check, and I called a number Kevin left me to call if I saw John. I called the number and told him John was here. That's all I know about that."

Jack asked Chuck if he ever saw Allison and Kevin together.

"No, but she had been late a few times and a no-show a couple of other times."

Jack asked if he knew anything about this video ring.

"I asked Kevin one time about this guy Fred and how he knew John. Kevin told me that people who ask too many questions usually regret it. He told me, 'Fred does his thing, and John does what he does. I do what I do, and you do as you're told. Don't ask a question you don't want the answer to.' I figured I was making $175,000 or so, and that's all I need to worry about."

Jack asked if he ever worried he was drug trafficking and committing a felony doing it.

"I was just taking items in and giving them to another person. I had nothing to do with distributing them to people."

The US attorney told Chuck that just for the part he played in this drug trafficking and possession of stolen property, he would normally be facing twenty years to life in prison. The US attorney asked him when the next delivery was coming to the restaurant.

Chuck said, "I just got one yesterday, and the guy will be coming to pick the packages up on Wednesday next week."

The US attorney also told Chuck that all of his phones would be bugged by the police, and he was not to make contact with anyone regarding this sting or it would be him the government would be waging war on.

Jack then asked if Rachael knew anything about all of this, and Chuck stated she had no idea, she just thought the restaurant was doing well.

Jack asked him about his relationship with Allison.

Chuck stated, "We didn't have a relationship. I admit I looked at the videos, and she was hot even for a young girl. I got a link from a friend of mine on how to sign up for the videos of Allison and hundreds of other girls from all over the country."

"Who was this friend?" Jack asked.

"A guy I have known for years, Ken Taylor."

Jack looked like he was going to be sick.

The US attorney told Chuck he needed to work his regular shifts at work and not to do anything differently than he had been doing.

Jack asked if Chuck knew where they might have taken John.

Chuck said, "Like I said before. I told you all I know about that."

The US attorney told him to look at the mug books to see if he could identify anyone he had seen during this time working for Tony Bolero. The US attorney stated that as long as Chuck participated until these people were arrested, he would give him the deal they were looking for. Then the US attorney told Chuck he was free to go for the day.

The meeting broke up, and Jack and the US attorney went into Jack's office. Jack thanked the US attorney for his help, and he told Jack, "If this gets ugly, you call me, and I'll call in the FBI." Jack told the U.S. attorney if he could speed up the DNA process it would certainly help finding the father of the fetus. The U.S. attorney stated he would make some calls to see what could be done. Jack thanked him but felt they would be fine.

Once the US attorney left, Jack almost fell into his chair after hearing the name of his stepdad being mentioned by these mobsters. Jack felt his stepdad was cheating on his mom by watching these videos. He was really undecided as to what to do or say to his stepdad. He was exhausted after being in this interview for several hours.

During the interview with Chuck, Jack got a call from Landon regarding the DNA sample. The message on his phone just said, "After thinking about this all night I decided I was not going to give a sample unless you get a court order." Jack figured this was not going to turn out well, and Landon must be the father to take such a stance on the issue. Jack called the DA's office asking them if he could get a court order for Landon's DNA. The district attorney's office stated that if Jack thought this DNA would prove Landon had murdered Allison, they would give him the court order, but if not they needed more evidence.

Jack said, "It certainly gives Landon a motive to kill her."

The DA replied, "Since there are so many people who already have a motive, we have to connect Landon directly to the murder. Or no court order."

Jack had no choice but to let this part of the case wait until they had more evidence to suggest Landon did it.

Jack and his team sat down after the US Attorney left to discuss all that was said in the meeting. Jack advised his team of the role Chuck would be playing going forward, and everyone needed to be ready to move the minute the packages were picked up at the restaurant. Jack told the team what to look for in these packages and the type of people they would be dealing with. Jack made sure all of his guys would be in full gear in case there were shots fired. He also told his team not to breathe a word of this to anyone since these bad guys might decide to take Chuck out of the equation in the meantime. He gave them the timeline that Chuck had stated regarding the packages being picked up next Wednesday. Jack asked if there were any questions, and the team all seemed to be on the same page. He told his team to get some rest over the weekend but be alert for anything out of the ordinary.

Saturday morning came very soon for Jack. As he sat at home having breakfast, he knew he needed to go speak to the Tuttle's and ask Paul to talk with Landon regarding the DNA sample. The one thing he couldn't deal with was the question this request was sure to be met with. Jack hoped the Tuttle's would understand he was just doing his job and trying to be as thorough as possible. After Jack got ready to go out the door, he called Paul to ask him if it would be all right if he stopped by. Paul told Jack it was fine for him to come by their home.

When Jack arrived, he rang the bell to be welcomed by Paul and Jennifer. They asked Jack in and offered him coffee, but he declined. Jack asked how they had been holding up, and they just stated it was not getting any easier, and they will welcome the news when he could tell them the killer of their daughter had been captured. Paul asked how they could help him. Jack began by saying they had a lot of new leads in Allison's case, but he couldn't go into any details since they were trying to keep these latest developments under wraps until things unfolded.

Paul asked Jack why he was beating around the bush. Jack stated that during their investigation, there had been some unlikely twists and turns in trying to find the father of Allison's baby. Jack explained the football team had been cleared, as well as Chuck from the restaurant, and of course Paul. But his Buccal DNA was only used to measure the panel against Allison's. Jack then said, "I called Landon to get a sample of his DNA to go along with yours so we could rule out people who had DNA strands close to the family's DNA."

Paul looked at Jack and just asked him flat out, "Are you suggesting Landon might be the baby's father?"

"We have to get his DNA since some of the DNA in a family is all very similar. But quite honestly, we need to eliminate him as a precaution. We're just trying to be very thorough in our investigation so we don't exclude any variances."

Jennifer asked if Jack wanted them to call Landon. He stated he called Landon, but he was not very obliging when it came to giving a DNA Buccal swab. He then said, "Yes, I'm asking you to call him and ask him to come in and give the swab."

Jennifer looked at Paul and back at Jack and said, "If it will help you find the killer, I will make the call."

Jack thanked them both for their time and assured them they were getting very close to finding this person or persons responsible and bringing them to justice. Jack asked Paul as he was preparing to leave, "I don't think I ever asked what kind of work Landon does?"

Paul answered, "He works for a large heating and cooling contractor in Charlotte."

"He drives to Charlotte every day?"

"No, he keeps the van at his place."

After Jack left the Tuttle's home, he remembered what the forensic people said about the fiberglass from the tape.

Since Landon works for a heating and cooling company, this also linked Landon to the crime. Jack was hoping in the back of his mind these two siblings didn't get some sick romance going, which led to Allison getting pregnant and Landon feeling like he had to kill her.

Jack was driving back to his home when he started thinking about his stepdad and the video list he was on. Jack pulled off the road to digest everything regarding the one man in this world who cared about him and raised him. He could not fathom how he was going to broach the subject, and he wondered what mentioning it to his stepdad would even do to help the case. He was sure bringing this out in the open to his mom would definitely put a strain on their marriage. He still felt his mom had a right to know her husband was getting his kicks watching underage girls. He decided just to drop by his mom's house to visit with her a little while.

Jack drove to his homeplace and the only real home he ever knew growing up. When he pulled up at the house, his mom, Linda, met him at the door and was so glad to see him. They hugged one another and got caught up on all of the small talk a mother and her child do when they are not visiting as much as either one of them would have liked. Jack asked where his stepdad was, and his mom said he was at the shop as usual.

Jack asked, "On a Saturday?"

His mom just shrugged her shoulders and said, "He's always there anymore."

"Is everything all right with both of you?"

"I guess, but not like it used to be. He's distracted with work or something."

Jack decided after he left his mom that he would stop by the shop to see what was so important. Jack and his mom chatted for an hour or so, and then Jack hugged his mom and gave her a kiss on the cheek. He left his mom and drove to the shop to see his stepdad.

When Jack pulled up at the shop, there were no signs his stepdad was doing any work since the doors were closed. Jack walked in the side door and was very quiet as he approached the office. Jack could hear something playing, like a television or radio, and when he peered in the edge of the door, he saw his stepdad looking at the computer. He stood there for a minute or so until he could hear moaning and noise familiar with a sex video.

Jack cleared his throat and said, "So that's what you're doing instead of being with mom."

His stepdad, Ken, said, "I didn't hear you come in."

Jack asked, "What are you doing?"

Ken said, "Me and Linda were not exactly burning up the bedroom lately."

"Maybe if you were at home and not watching young girls on the Internet, things might get better."

"What young girls?"

Jack said, "Allison Tuttle."

"Who?"

Jack replied, "Don't even bother lying to me. I know you watched the videos with Allison in them, and I have the e-mails to prove it."

"Where the hell do you get off spying on me?" Ken asked.

"You're a suspect in this homicide since your name is linked to these videos. So don't pretend you're not looking at these young girls. Why are you looking at girls this age anyway? Are you a pedophile?"

Ken stated he started watching these when he got an e-mail from a friend of his.

Jack said, "You need to stop this now before I have to arrest you."

"You'll arrest me?"

Jack replied, "I got my integrity growing up from you. What would you want me to do?"

Ken dropped his head in shame for having stooped to this level of degradation. He said, "I'm sorry, son. I never wanted it to come to this."

"Go home and wrap your arms around mom like you should be doing before you wind up in jail."

Ken asked if he had said anything to his mom.

Jack said, "Of course not. If you ever watch this crap again, I will not only tell her. I will show her your name on the list of suspects with the rest of the perverts and pedophiles."

Ken shook his head yes and told Jack he loved him.

Jack responded that he loved his stepdad also and left the building. He looked in his mirror as his stepdad left for home. He left his stepfather's shop, hoping he had heard the last of him looking at these young girls on this Internet site. Jack prayed his mother and his stepdad could work through their issues and get back to the loving family he remembered when he was growing up.

Jack started back home just to spend the rest of the afternoon relaxing, but he just couldn't get his mind off where John was, or if these thugs had actually killed him. He went by the restaurant and asked for the address where John lived. Jack decided to ride out by there and just look around. He knew that if he found anything, he would have to apply for a search warrant since John had been missing for some time.

As Jack arrived at John's address, he saw a very small run-down house that needed a lot of repair, and he noticed an old vehicle sitting nearby but clearly had not been running in quite sometime. The lawn was very high and in desperate need of a mower. He saw a run-down outbuilding that was nearly falling down out in the field. Jack just kind of looked around very cautiously when he noticed the back door was ajar. He pulled his pistol from its holster and crept close to the edge of the door just enough so he could see in. It was difficult to see since there was no light inside except for the sunlight coming in through the dirt-covered windows. Jack looked in and then gently pushed the door open, wide enough he could squeeze inside. With his pistol ready to fire, Jack stepped inside. He saw trash strewn everywhere, and the entire house was in a state of disarray. Jack started going from one room to the other until he had made sure the house was free of other people.

As Jack went from room to room, again looking for clues to the disappearance of John, he noticed a very dusty area on the table where John's computer clearly had been. He looked around and found other oddities. There were clearly other items missing from the home evidenced by the dust outline of where those items had been. In one corner of a bedroom, there was a dust outline of where a shotgun or rifle had stood at some point. There were outlines in a cabinet where some type of small boxes had been stored. As Jack looked around, he saw or actually didn't see a television, stereo, radio, or any other normal items like in most homes. He continued to look around without collecting anything, knowing he would need a warrant to take anything out of the home. Jack finally finished his search and walked back out of the house and into the sunlight outside.

Jack called the district attorney's office and left a message telling them he wanted a search warrant for John's property to look for clues in the death of Allison as well as the disappearance of John Gordon.

While Jack was in the area, he decided to try to speak with anyone living near John, so he stopped at a neighbor's house right down the road. He got out of his cruiser as a man stepped out on his porch and asked him what he wanted. Jack advised the man he was a detective with the police department and was investigating the disappearance of John Gordon. The man asked what that had to do with him. Jack stated he wanted to check with the man to see when was the last time he had seen John. The man just stated he had nothing to do with John.

Jack asked if he ever noticed any activity at John's house.

The man replied, "There were some strange things going on at that house."

Jack asked what kind of things, and the man stated there are people coming in and out all hours of the night. He went on to say that John has some very rich friends by the cars he sees at the house. Jack asked when the last time he saw a car there, and the man responded a few days ago. He thanked the man for his time and told him to have a good day.

Jack got back in his cruiser and was headed home when Jennifer Tuttle called him. After a few minutes of chit-chatting, she told Jack she had spoken to Landon. After a long conversation, she had talked Landon into giving up his DNA by telling him she had to go down and give hers to the medical examiner anyway. She told Jack they would be down on Monday. Jack told her that they really didn't need hers, but he thanked her for working with Landon to get his sample. She told Jack she wanted to give hers just so Landon thinks hers was required also to complete the DNA panel for the family. Jack agreed and told her he would see both of them on Monday. Jack hung up the phone and went home for the day.

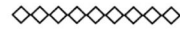

On Sunday, October 20, Jack got out of bed and went outside to get his newspaper like every other Sunday. Jack's mom called and asked him to come over for lunch today, and he agreed. When Jack arrived, his mother gave him the biggest hug and told him everything was so much better since Ken was now coming home in the evening and seemed more interested in her like he did years ago. Jack was very pleased to hear those words from her. After lunch, Ken and Jack walked outside wherein Ken told Jack he was very thankful for him, and he hoped Jack could forgive him for being weak. Jack hugged his stepdad and just told him he was glad he and his mom were back on good terms. Ken asked if he was still a suspect, and Jack told him everyone on that list was a suspect, and he still might have to come down to the station for questioning at some point.

Ken said, "Please try to keep me out of it. It would kill your mom."

Jack replied, "You should have thought of that before you did it. I won't hinder the investigation. It takes me where it takes me. Is there anything you're not telling me about this whole thing with Allison?"

"Jack, no, you can't believe I had anything to do with that."

"I would like to think otherwise, but I owe it to the family to find out what happened and to bring the people who did this to justice."

"I admit I looked at the videos, but that's it." About that time Jack's mom came outside and said, "Everything is perfect today. Both my guys are here."

Jack smiled and hugged his mom.

About 4:00 p.m., Jack told his mom he was leaving since he had a long day tomorrow. She asked if Jack was all right, and he just said, "We are getting much closer to finding the killer, but it is going to bring a lot of people out in the light."

Linda asked her son what he meant by that.

He answered, "There are lots of people in this town who have been hiding a dark secret. That's all I can say." Jack hugged his parents again and left going home.

When Jack opened his eyes on Monday morning, October 21, he was ready to hopefully bring some closure to the Tuttle family that week since he knew the pickup with Chuck would be going off on Wednesday. He also knew Jennifer and Landon would be coming to the station to give DNA, and he was going to get a search warrant for John's property. Jack was thinking it has been fourteen days since Allison was found dead. Jack had a good feeling about where some of these things were going to lead and that by the weekend, they may even have the killer in custody. Jack had his breakfast and got dressed for work.

Jack arrived at his office and went in to meet with his staff to have their regular Monday meeting to recap the events from the prior week. He and his team went over all of the evidence and the suspects thus far. They also went over the DNA evidence regarding the baby and the medical examiner's findings. Jack bounced a few ideas off the team to see if they had any comments either way regarding Landon.

Jack said, "The DNA panel showed, of course, Paul was Allison's dad and, therefore, was very similar to the DNA of Allison. The medical examiner's office stated the baby's DNA shows the father is a family member of the Tuttle's. So does it make sense that if the DNA would have to come from another family member it would have to be Landon's baby?"

One of the other investigators spoke up and said, "What if it turns out to be a cousin or uncle or something?"

Jack stated, "The M.E. told me it would have to be a male blood relative." Jack advised his team of what was taking place today regarding Jennifer and Landon giving their DNA, as well as reminding them about the thing with Chuck on Wednesday. Jack asked if anyone had anything to add, and one of the team members spoke up and said, "Do we have any other information regarding John's disappearance?"

Jack said he had called the DA's office asking for a search warrant for John's residence. "When we get the warrant, we need to get out there also."

The meeting broke up just as Jennifer and Landon was coming in to give their DNA.

Jack welcomed the two and thanked them for being willing to help them find Allison's killer and took them over to the forensic office to give the swab. Jack left them with a team member and headed back to his office. Jack had numerous messages to return since he had been so busy, and he had not had time to return calls that were not related to this case. Jack finished his tasks and was told the warrant had arrived for John's place. Jack grabbed his team and headed off to John's for the investigation.

When the team arrived at John's house, they spread out and started looking around outside in case they found any evidence or clues around the perimeter of the house. This took a while longer than normal since the grass was so high, and there were so many places a person could hide something, as well as the possibility someone could have dropped a clue or piece of evidence. The team also searched around the dilapidated car both inside and out. The old building on the property was also searched for clues. The investigators also found a place in the wooded area nearby where someone was perfecting their shooting skills by firing at targets, bottles, and cans. This area had lots of activity, showing someone had been using this firing range for several months. The investigators found some shell casings and empty shotgun shells, so they bagged those for prints as well. The team took photos of the area and the targets.

One of the investigators got a metal detector out of one of the cruisers and started going around the property as well. He got a lot of false readings with beer cans and other metal and aluminum items. The metal detector sounded again, but this time it had detected something different. The investigator shouted for Jack, and when Jack asked what he had, the investigator said it was something solid, but it was down in the high grass. So Jack came over. The investigator and Jack dug where the detector was beeping, and they found a piece of jewelry that looked to be genuine gold. The whole team then started looking in the area to see if there was any more jewelry or other items. Once the team finished this area, they immediately started looking nearer to the house and the paths going in and out in hopes of finding another clue.

The team then moved their search into the house itself. They began by opening some curtains and blinds, allowing more light to enter the house. The team spread out to cover more area and looked into every nook and cranny to find more clues. The forensic team did find dozens of fingerprints but were only able to lift about half since the house and the areas were so dusty and dirty. The team took a complete set of photos showing where each print was taken from. The team also took samples from the cabinet where the packages had been at some time, hoping to find traces of drugs. They then found a storage area in the floor of the bedroom under a throw rug. The space in the floor was empty except for a partial roll of duct tape, similar to the duct tape used on Allison Tuttle. The team took the tape back to the lab for comparison analysis and was also able to get some additional fingerprints from the floor slats. One of the team members tapped on the ceiling and the other floor areas, looking to find another hidden storage. Once the team had finished their investigation of the house, they took all of their forensic evidence and the jewelry back to the lab.

On the way back to the station, Jack started thinking about John Gordon as the potential murderer. Jack was thinking through the evidence and other factual information against John thus far:

1. John was probably the last person to see Allison alive the night she disappeared.
2. John admitted he and Allison had argued in front of people at the restaurant.
3. John pawned the expensive diamond earrings.
4. John testified he saw the earrings on Allison the night she disappeared.
5. John's fingerprints were found on Allison's car.
6. John's alibi was he was at work the night Allison disappeared and then went home.
7. Tape found hidden at John's house is similar to the tape used to bind the hands of Allison
8. John had a thing for Allison
9. John could have been the baby's father

He was thinking that if this tape proves to be the same as the one used to bind Allison's hands, this could very well prove John was the murderer. Jack also thought the only problem with that theory was the prime suspect is still missing. He was hoping the fingerprints from John's house will produce some insight as to John's other rich friends that the neighbor told Jack about. Jack arrived back at the station with his team to turn the evidence over to the lab, and the medical examiner to have the tape tested. Jack was excited to see where the whole thing on Wednesday was going to go. He knew, if nothing else, arresting some of these people running these drugs may produce more suspects as well as give Jack's team an opportunity to shut down a true criminal enterprise.

Jack also had other suspects running in his mind. There was Kevin, who, according to John, had given the expensive diamond earrings to Allison in the first place. During the same testimony, John said that Allison went to Kevin when he came into the restaurant. Jack also thought of Fred, another man coming into the restaurant who had taken a fancy to Allison, and vice versa. Once again, during John's testimony, he indicated that Allison and Fred had talked about the videos of Allison on the Internet. Jack still felt John was the key suspect for the murder, and right now he was convinced Landon would turn out to be the father of Allison's baby.

Once Jack and the team got back to the station, he was hoping to get the results from the swab given this morning. But since the medical examiner did not work exclusively for this department, but rather for the entire county, he had been called out of the office on another case.

Since it was after lunch, Jack decided he would go to the restaurant to eat. When Jack arrived, he saw pretty much the same faces he had seen each time he had been to the restaurant. One of the waitresses came over to take Jack's order, and they exchanged greetings. While a local man started chatting with him about different things like two old friends would do. This encounter made Jack realize how much he loved working in this small town. Jack found it refreshing to have a conversation without the man asking dozens of questions surrounding the murder of Allison. As Jack was about to leave, Chuck came into the restaurant, and he spoke to him, asking how he liked his lunch. So to the patrons, everything between Jack and Chuck appeared to be back to normal. Jack paid his bill and left to go back to the station.

On the way back, Jack went by the Tuttle's house to check up on them. When he rang the doorbell, Jennifer answered the door and welcomed Jack inside. Since Paul was not there at the time, Jennifer and Jack went into the living room and sat down. The two began talking, but it was lots of small talk. Finally, Jack looked at her and asked how the family was holding up. She told Jack that everything was very strained between all of the family. He told her he was sorry but reassured her that everything possible was being done to find the killer. She said she knew the department was doing everything they could, and the family appreciated their hard work. She added that the house was very quiet now even when the three of them were home.

Jack asked about Lisa, and Jennifer just said she is not the same either. Jennifer said that the one thing that might bring the family together again is finding out who did this to their daughter.

Then Jennifer asked Jack, "Have you gotten the results from Landon's DNA?"

Jack answered, "No, the medical examiner was out of the office on another case and had not been there to run the samples."

Jennifer told Jack she was praying so hard the sample won't prove Landon is the father. Jack told her he understood but not to stress out over this until the results are in.

She said, "It would kill Paul to find out our son was the father of Allison's baby."

Jack tried to calm her nerves by saying, "The one thing about this job that I don't think I'll ever get used to is the fact that people you are closest to have things going on in their lives that sometimes get out of control. When I think I've seen it all, I can't help but be amazed at how much I really didn't know them as much as I thought I did. Everyone thinks their mom is just their mom, and the same for their dad and their extended family, but we never stop to think these people have all sorts of backgrounds and sometimes skeletons in their closets also. I have learned not to judge people by their actions, but to learn from their mistakes."

Jennifer thanked Jack for sharing those thoughts but wondered why he would say this to her. She asked what he was trying to tell her.

Jack said, "Jennifer, I hate to tell you this, but I have been putting off this conversation until I had all of the facts. Allison was posing in videos and putting these videos on the Internet."

Jennifer looked at Jack with a hurt he could see in her eyes.

She asked, "What kind of videos?"

Jack told her they were very risqué videos, showing Allison and another young woman doing sexual things to one another.

Jennifer started crying, and Jack felt awful having to tell her these things.

Jack told her that he didn't want her to hear about this in the newspaper or from the television. Jennifer asked "What, were these, sex videos?"

Jack said, "The sex that was in the video was just of Allison and a woman having oral sex with one another and using sex toys."

"Oh my God," Jennifer said. She asked what else.

"The videos were put on an Internet website and sold to men all over the world. I hate to lay this on you, but I knew Paul would have a heart attack if he knew this was going on."

Jennifer told Jack that Allison must have been forced to do these things.

"She was drugged on one of the videos, but clearly she did this on her own."

She asked if he was sure she did this voluntarily.

"If I wasn't sure, I wouldn't be bringing this to you." Jack was hugging Jennifer to give her some comfort.

She said, "My God, I had no idea."

Jack told her he had no idea either, but it had come up during the investigation.

"What in the world would make her do such a thing?" Jennifer asked.

Jack stated, "It looked like she wanted all the things in her life, and she decided to use these videos to get the money to buy things."

Jennifer asked, "Was she having sex for money?"

"I haven't found any proof of that. It looked like she fell in with some people who prey on young girls and exploit their need or desire for money."

Jennifer was certainly shocked to hear these things from Jack.

Jack told her that the department was currently running down the owners of these websites. Jennifer remarked that when Paul finds out, he'll be devastated.

Jack just said, "That's what I hate about this job. Good people are hurt so badly by the actions of others. I hope you understand why I told you. You had a right to know these things." He hugged her and left.

Once Jack left, Jennifer could not help but think Jack was so right. And the situation with Allison was one where she got mixed up with some people she never should be acquainted with. Allison wound up pregnant and for some unknown reason was found dead. Jennifer knew now that Allison was probably going to tell her what was going on the night she went missing. She thought it must be what Allison meant when she said she wanted to tell her everything. Jennifer started to think about her own past and the things she used to do growing up. Jennifer just started crying, feeling like she was not there for her daughter when she needed her most.

Jack felt bad about having to tell this grieving mother that her daughter was engaged in these activities. As he was driving home, he kept thinking this family had always been a beacon for the community, and here they were going through all of this. And also when these criminals are brought up on charges, everyone in the area and the country would know about this family's pain. The very community this family had stood by all these years will be condemning them for their daughter's indiscretions. Jack arrived at home and turned in for the evening.

Meanwhile, at the Tuttle house, Paul had come home to find Jennifer weeping. Jennifer told him she had something to tell him. He asked where Lisa was, and Jennifer told him she had asked one of Lisa's friend's moms if she could spend the night with them. Jennifer told Paul he better sit down. She began by telling her husband that Jack had been here earlier, telling her a story about their daughter. Paul sat listening to his wife while she filled Paul in to what their daughter was doing with her life. Paul was shocked to hear such things about his daughter.

At one point, Paul stood up and said, "No, Allison did not do these things and I am not listening to this anymore."

Jennifer told him to sit down.

Paul sat back down as his wife went over all of the details and why Jack thought she was doing these things. Paul said, "If she needed money, she could have come to us."

Jennifer said, "Don't you get it? It wasn't about the money. It was her doing things to rebel against our button-down lifestyle. We were so busy trying to solve everyone else's problems, we neglected our own family's problems."

Paul dropped his head as he just sat near his wife in disbelief. He finally just said, "What have I done?"

Jennifer told him it was not his fault; it was something inside Allison.

Paul asked, "God, why would you allow such a thing inside this God-fearing household. We have been your servants for so many years, yet our daughter was allowed to stray so far from her path."

Jennifer hugged her husband and just said, "I didn't see this in her, and I'm her mother. I must be a poor excuse for a mother."

Paul looked at his wife and said, "You are a terrific mother, and you are not to blame yourself."

Then Jennifer told her husband there was one more thing he needed to know. She then said, "Landon and I went to the police station today and gave a DNA sample for the purpose of making sure Landon is not the baby's father."

Paul said, "I thought this was just to clear up the DNA panel."

"We had to tell you something. It was really to make sure Landon and Allison had not had sex since the panel showed it must be a male family member."

Paul looked like he had been run over by a truck. Jennifer told him the tests were not back yet.

The couple sat quietly for a while until Paul told his wife he couldn't be the pastor of this church anymore or any other church. He said, "How can I lead a flock and look them in the eye on a daily basis when my own family had fallen victim to the devil's wrath. I'm calling an emergency meeting of the church's administrative staff and steering committee where I will resign." Paul then said, "When all of this comes out, the church will be ruined."

Jennifer said, "See, even now you're only thinking of how this affects the church."

Paul told his wife she was right and that was the main reason he needed to leave the church. Paul said, "I have to take care of my family in this time of need. You will need me more than ever when all of this hits the newspapers and television."

Jennifer told her husband this was why she fell in love with him, and that he was the kindest, gentlest man she had ever known. "I too was a young woman once with a lot of issues I wanted to tell my mom about but was afraid of making her hate me. So it was easier to keep them to myself."

"And look how you turned out."

Jennifer just cracked a slight grin. The couple sat there, holding one another for several hours until well after midnight, when they went off to bed.

On Tuesday morning, October 22, Paul and his wife went through the motions of getting their day started, but there was very little conversation between them. Jennifer called Lisa at her friend's house and spoke to her for quite sometime, letting her know how much she loved her. Lisa asked if everything was all right, and her mom told her she just wanted to make sure she knew how much she was loved. Lisa said, "Are you ok?" Her mom just said she wanted her

An All-American Girl

to know she could tell her mom anything and got off the phone. Paul called the deacons of the church and asked them to call an emergency meeting. He walked over to his wife and hugged her for the longest time.

Across town, Jack got up and headed for his office as usual, when he got a call from Chuck. Chuck stated he had gotten a call from Kevin last night to make sure everything was set for Wednesday's pickup. Jack asked if that was their normal practice, and Chuck stated that Kevin usually just has the guy stop by to make the pickup, but this was the first time he had called. Jack had the feeling something was wrong for this guy to suddenly change the way this had been handled in the past. Jack asked what else the two of them talked about, and Chuck told him that Kevin asked if everything was all right at the restaurant. Chuck said, "Yes, why do you ask?" Kevin said he just wanted to make sure. Jack asked if he had mentioned this to anyone. Chuck said he had not told anyone anything. Jack asked him where he was right now, and Chuck said he was still at home and that his manager had opened the restaurant. Jack told him to stay there, and he would be right over. Chuck said, "Hold on a minute, someone is at the door." Jack could hear some noise in the background and radioed the other officers to meet him at Chuck's home immediately.

Jack was afraid this was also what happened to John. Someone had leaked the information about him being picked up by the police, and it got him killed. Jack turned on his siren and headed for Chuck's house.

When Jack arrived at Chuck's house, the front door was standing wide open, and there were no signs of Chuck. Jack drew his gun and got out of his cruiser. A few seconds later, the other officers pulled up and jumped out of their cruisers with guns drawn as well. Jack directed some of them to go around back and surround the house. Jack and his team carefully started moving toward the house. Jack and two of his other investigators were the first ones to go inside. The team carefully cleared the house room by room. There were clearly signs of a struggle. The phone was still off the hook, but Chuck was nowhere to be found.

The team went to Chuck's neighbor's houses to see if they had seen anyone at Chuck's in the last few minutes. Finally, one neighbor told the team they had seen a car there just before Detective Jack arrived. Jack asked him to describe the vehicle and if he saw which way the car was headed when it drove off. The neighbor told Jack the car was headed away from town, and they immediately got the information out over the radio. Several of the officers there with Jack screamed off in the distance and headed in the same direction. Jack asked if he happened to see the license plate, but the neighbor just had eye surgery and could not make out the number. Jack asked if he could identify any of the people in the car, but he told Jack he couldn't see them that well. Jack thanked him for the information.

Jack and the other officers stayed at the house, looking for clues. Jack then thought about the packages at the restaurant, so he and another officer took off for the restaurant but left some officers behind at the house.

Jack and the officer arrived at the restaurant and went inside. They spoke to the waitress on duty and told her they were there to look around the office. While Jack looked for the packages in the office, the other officer looked in the cooler. Jack opened all of the lockers and asked the waitress if anyone other than Chuck had carried anything out of the office. The waitress stated a man had been by, but he picked up a cooler out of the walk-in, but that was earlier.

Jack asked her to describe the man.

The waitress gave a description of the man who picked up the cooler.

Jack asked, "Can you identify the man?"

She said she would try but really wasn't paying that much attention.

"Were there any of the regular customers here when the man came in and got the cooler?"

She stated some of the early morning customers may have still been here, but they were gone now.

Jack asked if any of them used a credit card, and she stated one of the men does pay by credit card every day. Jack got her to give him the information from the card receipt. The other officer came back from the walk in and told Jack there was nothing in it but food. Jack thanked the waitress but told her she needed to go with the officer to look at mug shots to see if she could recognize the guy. The waitress stated she could not leave the restaurant.

Jack told her that a man's life is at stake, and she went with the officer after telling the waitress just coming in what happened.

Jack called his office and gave them the information from the credit card receipt. Jack radioed his team to see if there was any sign of the vehicle from Chuck's, but no one had seen the car anywhere. Jack told them to keep looking. They put out a locate bulletin to other law enforcement to look for a car matching the description they had gotten from Chuck's neighbor. Jack got a radio call from the station giving him the cardholder's address from the receipt. He headed off to see if this man could identify the man who picked up the cooler.

When Jack arrived at the cardholder's home, he rang the bell. A man came to the door, and Jack asked if he was the person from the credit card receipt, and the man stated he was. Jack asked if he could come in, and the man told him he could. The detective introduced himself and then asked the man if he remembered seeing a man earlier at the restaurant picking up a cooler and carrying it out. The man stated he did see a man doing that, and he thought it was odd seeing someone carrying an entire cooler out of a restaurant. The man went on to say that he actually held the door open for the man to leave. Jack asked if he could identify the man, and the customer stated he definitely could. Jack asked if he would mind coming to the station with him and look at the mug books to find the man. The customer told Jack he would be glad to. Then Jack asked if he happened to see the vehicle the man put the cooler into, and he described the vehicle perfectly. Jack and the man left for the station at that point.

They arrived at the station where the waitress was already looking through the mug books. While the waitress was looking through the books, the man Jack had brought in went to the restroom, and on his way back, he passed a bulletin board with a wanted list on it. When he saw a photo of the man on the board, he immediately went to Jack. He told Jack that he had seen a photo of the guy at the restaurant. Jack asked where, and the man took him to the bulletin board and showed him the wanted poster. He took the poster down and asked him again if he was sure, and the man stated that was absolutely the guy who picked up the cooler. Jack took the poster and showed it to the waitress, and she too identified the guy on it right away. He thanked the two witnesses for their help and had officers take them back home. Jack looked at the photo of Kevin Michaels: a man on the SBI, State Bureau of Investigation, most wanted list. He could not believe this guy was seen in the area.

Jack called all of his team into his office and made them aware of who they were looking for and dealing with. Jack told the team, "This guy is wanted in several states for crimes against nature, drug smuggling, suspicion of murder, and several homicides." Jack also told the team he is most likely a player in the disappearance of John Gordon and Chuck from the restaurant and is one of Tony Bolero's guys as well as a guy named Fred. Jack stated Michaels is presumed to be armed and dangerous. Jack told the team he had to call the SBI for this guy. He told the team to be on the lookout for these guys and to have APBs issued on the car where the man from the restaurant had seen the man loading the cooler into.

Jack called the SBI, spoke to one of their investigators, and informed him that there had been a positive sighting of Kevin Michaels in the area in the last twelve hours. The SBI investigator told Jack they were on their way to assist in the capture of this guy. Jack advised his team that the SBI were on their way to the station for an update on this criminal.

During the time Jack and the team were waiting for the SBI to show up, he had been in touch with the medical examiner regarding the DNA for Jennifer and Landon. Jack was told Jennifer of course matched the DNA profile panel from Allison. Then he was told that Landon's DNA was a panel match for Allison as far as being a relative, but he was not the baby's father. Jack could not believe what he had just heard. Jack asked if the medical examiner was sure, and he told Jack that Landon was absolutely not the baby's father. Jack had also gotten the administrative staff to prepare a book for each SBI investigator, showing the evidence thus far, as well as the known associates from the beginning of the Allison Tuttle case. Jack had to get off the phone when the SBI walked into his office.

The SBI introduced themselves to Jack and then asked if there was a meeting room where everyone could be brought up to speed on both sides. The SBI chief investigator, Tom Morgan, began by telling Jack's team what they knew about Kevin Michaels and the terrible crimes he was involved with, as well as the murders they believed he had a part in. Tom also told everyone about this guy being involved with crimes against nature with minors and drug smuggling.

The SBI had been after this guy for over a year, but every time they got close, he moved into another area and set up camp there. Tom said they used the term *camp* since he is only in a place for a short time before moving. Tom also indicated that Kevin had been on everyone's radar, from the US attorney down to the local law enforcement all over the southeast. The only reason the FBI was not involved was because Kevin kept his criminal activities confined to one state and had not been caught shipping drugs over state lines. Tom stated that Kevin had been in prison numerous times, and each time he was released, he went right back to doing the same type of crime and was getting better at not getting caught.

Jack and his team were absorbing all information from Tom with great interest.

Tom stated, "A criminal like Kevin Michaels is not only smart, but he surrounds himself with career criminals like Tony Bolero and others. When Kevin feels us coming after him, we believe he kills off the local people he used to set up his criminal activities so there are no loose ends." Tom continued, "He is definitely armed and dangerous and will stop at nothing to get away, so be prepared for a firefight." Tom asked if there were any questions.

Several of Jack's team asked questions about his patterns and known associates.

Tom answered the questions the best he could but said, "From the sounds of things going on here, you guys know more about that than we do right now." With that remark, Tom stated that if there were no more questions, he would turn the briefing over to Detective Jack Williams for his guys to take notes.

Detective Jack Williams introduced himself to the SBI investigators and began by telling the story of Allison Tuttle. Jack told the SBI he had prepared a book of the case thus far to bring each of them up to speed. He told them about the activity surrounding the nude videos posted on the Internet and how that alone had progressed into some type of criminal sex ring in the area with the videos being posted by someone, and memberships being sold on a national level. He then told the team about this Fred character who appeared on the scene and took up with Allison. Jack mentioned John Gordon as a small-time criminal and how he fit into this criminal puzzle. Jack talked about the expensive diamond earrings given to Allison from Kevin Michaels and then pawned by John. He informed them about Chuck's role in all of the smuggling, and how he became involved and for the reason Chuck stated—money. Jack continued by telling about the deposition John had given before the district attorney's office and the phone call where John was going to meet Fred and was never heard from again. Jack then went through Chuck's arrest and his testimony to the US attorney and his willingness to work with the police to allow them to intercept the pickup of the drugs from the restaurant on Wednesday of this week. He then brought them up to speed as to what transpired today to thwart those efforts and escalated this to another level. Jack mentioned the kidnapping today of Chuck and the call from Kevin to Chuck prior to the kidnapping. Jack then went over all of the evidence collected thus far. He asked if there were any questions from the SBI team, and they went through the questions one by one. The briefing was then turned over to the forensic specialist for better information.

Once the forensic specialist was done giving the information thus far, as well as answering all the questions the SBI team had for him, Tom asked Jack if the two of them could speak in private.

Once the two investigators shut the door to Jack's office, Tom told Jack, "You know of course the leak came from your office, right?"

"Why do you believe that?" Jack responded.

"John Gordon was here, and he's dead. Chuck was here, and he's dead."

Jack said, "We have not confirmed either one of them are dead."

"They're dead, I guarantee it. These guys don't take prisoners. They kill everyone expendable and move on. There must be someone still here who works with these guys. We just have to find out who it is before they're gone again. It's someone you've overlooked. Think, Jack, who seemed to not be involved when you interviewed them but is in deep with these guys."

An All-American Girl

Jack thought for a bit, and the only person he could think of was Rachael.

Tom asked how she fit into this thing, and Jack told him about her coming in and crying, saying she was the wife of Chuck. Tom asked for Chuck's last name, and Jack gave him the full name.

Tom made a telephone call and walked back over to Jack and said, "Chuck was not married." Jack thought back to the interview where Rachael was crying, saying she needed a good divorce lawyer. Jack asked Tom what their next move should be. Tom stated he thought the best thing to do would be to wait until morning and then launch an all-out blitz to find Kevin and Tony.

Jack said, "Forgive me, but I don't agree." He called the US attorney on his cell phone and asked him for his help.

The US attorney got a federal APB for the vehicles that had been identified by the witnesses. Jack got off the phone and advised Tom what the US attorney had done. The two investigators decided to let the APB do the leg work and see what that yields. Jack went home for the night, and the SBI guys went to a hotel nearby.

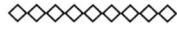

While the investigators slept, the APB was working overtime, and the Virginia State Highway Patrol stopped a vehicle matching the description of the one used to transport the cooler from the restaurant. The occupants were detained until the local authorities in charge of the case were contacted. A call had gone out to the US attorney's office in Greenville, NC, and a message was left to call the precinct in Virginia where the occupants were being held.

When the US attorney's office opened on Wednesday, October 24, the assistant played the messages, wrote down the information, and placed it on the US attorney's desk. When the US attorney came in, he immediately called Jack and advised him there had been two men detained during the night in Martinsville, VA, after they were stopped in a vehicle that matched the description they had been given. The US attorney told Jack he would read him the exact message: "At 3:41 a.m., two white males were detained by VHP, Virginia Highway Patrol officers in the city of Martinsville, VA. The men were identified as Jimmy Martin Little and George no middle name Gentry and are being held at the Martinsville, VA, detention center."

Jack thanked the US attorney for his help and got off the phone. Jack then turned to Tom and said, "You were wrong. John Gordon, a.k.a. Jimmy Little, is alive and in custody in Martinsville, VA. He and another man, George Gentry, were stopped by the VHP in the car used to transport the cooler from the restaurant. Want to go for a ride?"

Tom said, "I've got a better idea. Why don't you ride with me?"

Jack agreed, and in about fifteen minutes, they stopped at the airport in Winston-Salem, NC, and boarded a helicopter to carry them to Martinsville, VA.

The two investigators landed in Martinsville, VA, and were met by a representative of the Martinsville, VA, Police Department to transport the men to the detention center. Once inside, the investigators were in a holding cell when Jimmy and George were brought in. When John, a.k.a. Jimmy, came into the cell, he could not believe it was Jack.

Jack said, "Hi, John."

John just nodded his head.

Jack said to George, "I don't believe we've had the pleasure."

"Allow me," Tom said. "This is George Gentry, a.k.a. Harry Jones, Kevin Michael's cousin. Harry, Harry, Harry, didn't you promise a DA in Mecklenburg County, NC, that you were not going to get in trouble again?"

Harry said, "We weren't doing anything when they stopped us."

"Your car was used to transport drugs from Chuck's restaurant," Tom said.

"No, it wasn't."

"Oh, but it was. We have witnesses who put the car there and the cooler loaded into the car by Kevin."

Harry remarked, "Oh my God, he set me up."

Then Jack said, "John, I thought you disappeared and was dead."

John replied, "He knew something bad was going to happen to him, so he went over to a friend's house to avoid anything happening."

"Honor among thieves, huh. Well, I think it's obvious that you can't go back to Kevin. So what do we do with you? Obviously, Kevin used the car, hoping you two geniuses would be caught to throw us off. And look where we are." Jack looked at John and said, "Something still bothers me about you and Heather. You guys trashed Allison in your e-mails back and forth, yet you played up to her face. What's the deal with that?"

John said, "Allison was very pretty, and she thought she was so untouchable. Yet here she was stripping for people she didn't even know."

"So you and Heather were jealous of Allison. You, since she wouldn't sleep with you, and Heather, because she wanted to be Allison."

"I knew other people were having sex with her, so why not me?"

Jack responded, "You're sounding more and more like the killer."

John said, "I did not kill her."

"Then how did you come to have the diamond earrings you pawned?"

John started to speak and then paused briefly.

Jack warned, "Don't lie to me, or I'll convict you of this murder. I have enough evidence to arrest and convict you."

"I lied about Allison wearing the earrings that night. Allison had given them to Heather along with some clothing to hide for her. Heather called me and told me she had the earrings."

Jack asked why she would call him.

John said, "Heather and I had been seeing one another without her mom knowing it. I wasn't really into Heather until I had met with her one night, and she came on to me, so we had sex. After that, she bugged me all the time like we were a couple or something. We'd go out and wind up either at my place or in her attic, having sex. I told Heather I needed some money really bad, so she gave me the earrings to pawn. She was going to tell Allison that she had loaned them out to a friend and would get them back. When I took off, I never went back to get the earrings."

"So you and Heather were just having sex? That explains why she was so mad about talking to me because she thought I knew about you two and was going to ask her about it in front of her mother."

John said, "Probably. And there was no way she wanted her mom to know about me and her, and certainly not that we were having sex."

"I have to get her back in here to question her again." Jack said.

Since neither of these two guys were Harvard attorneys, the two investigators decided to use a tactic to gain their assistance.

Jack said, "You transported a vehicle used to transport drugs over the state line. Tom, you're the expert here. What is the maximum penalty for that?"

Tom said, "I'm sure we can get them on other charges as well, so I'd say they are looking at twelve years in a maximum security prison, where they are surely to get stabbed to death by someone with a debt owed to Kevin."

John spoke up, "We'll take our chances in court."

Jack remarked, "Good thinking. Officer, transport these guys back to Winston-Salem, NC, and place them in the local detention center, where they are sure to meet someone Kevin knows."

The two guys looked at one another as the officer led them toward the door.

John said, "Hey, Jack, what do you want from us?"

"Kevin Michaels."

George said, "No way."

Jack said, "Good luck, you guys."

John asked, "What do we get in return?"

Jack spoke to Tom privately and then told John, "If your information leads to the arrest of Kevin Michaels, Fred, Adam, William Thacker, and the video ring, a walk on all counts and witness protection."

John and George talked for a few minutes and then decided they would rather take a chance with the cops than with Kevin. They accepted the offer.

Jack said, "Just one more thing. What happened to Chuck?"

John answered, "Haven't seen him."

"No Chuck, no deal."

"Outside of town, there is an old run-down house off Highway 66 before you get to the big church on the left. You look in the old well."

Jack called his team and had them go out to this area and find the house and call him back with their findings. After thanking the law enforcement personnel in Martinsville for their terrific work, the two investigators took John and George back with them to North Carolina. On their way back to Winston-Salem, Jack received a call from his team, who advised him Chuck's body was in the well just like John said.

When the men landed back in Winston-Salem, Jack told Tom that the body was located in the exact location John described. Tom told John he passed the first test by showing them where Chuck's body was. Tom then asked John how he knew Chuck's body was there if he had nothing to do with it.

John responded, "I know these guys and how they work."

Tom and Jack both knew from that statement they may be on the right track to find and arrest these criminals.

John and George were taken to Jack's station house for further questioning.

On the way to the station, John and George told Jack they were hungry. The investigators stopped by a local burger joint. John wanted to get a sandwich and ordered for both him and George. When the sandwiches came out, they all headed off to the station.

Once they arrived at the station, they all went inside into an interrogation cell. While the suspects ate their sandwiches, Jack and Tom went into the former's office to prepare for the interviews. When the investigators came back out of the office, they walked in the holding cell and asked John, "You need to tell us more about this operation."

John told them he just did.

Tom looked confused and asked John what he meant.

George said, "The burger joint we just stopped at is one of the places where the drops are made."

Jack said, "You're kidding me."

John remarked, "They get a drop every week on Thursday, and it's picked up on Monday."

Tom asked, "You're positive?"

George assured, "I guarantee it."

Jack questioned, "Who delivers it?"

John answered, "Fred."

Tom said, "That's tomorrow. We have to get ready."

John spoke up, "I used to make the drop myself, and I know where the drop came from. Why don't you stake out the pickup point and the drop?"

Tom said, "Kevin will bolt now that the heat is on."

John commented, "You're crazy. He makes a fortune off the drop there. He'll have Fred make the drop. But if you pinch Fred, you'll never get Kevin."

Jack remarked, "He's right. Why don't we stake out the pickup point and the drop and follow Fred back to Kevin?"

John said, "He won't go to Kevin's as he will be in Charlotte on Thursday. He's always there on Thursday. That's when the swag, a term used by criminals that usually relates to stolen jewelry, comes into Charlotte. About a hundred thousand dollars worth comes into the airport through a courier service. You know one of those courier services. Man, you guys don't know shit about this operation."

Jack asked, "What about the sex videos?"

George stated, "That operation is run by Kevin and Adam."

Tom asked for Adam's last name.

George answered, "I don't know and don't want to know. He is a bad man. I heard he has killed a dozen or so of the women who wouldn't do what he told them to."

Tom asked George how they could get to Adam.

"Do you remember when those cops got killed in Maryland that was part of the prostitution ring?"

"Yes."

"That's Adam's signature move. Adam shipped some girls into the United States from overseas, and when some of them refused to prostitute for him, he killed like thirty of those women at one time. He took them out in a field and shot them while the others had to watch."

Tom asked how he knew.

George said, "Kevin was there, and he told me Adam was crazy and not to ever cross him and for me to never cross Adam either. He would kill you just to have something to do."

Jack asked if they knew who killed Allison.

John answered, "My money is on Adam."

Jack said, "Oh, by the way, you volunteered to take a DNA swab so we can match it to Allison's baby's DNA."

"Go ahead, it's not mine."

Tom and Jack told the men to sit tight; they were going to have a private word. Jack and Tom went into Jack's office and called their teams in to fill them in on what was happening.

Jack and Tom went over how each of the criminals were involved and what part they played in the criminal empire. They also informed the teams that the local burger joint is one of the drug houses, and there are large amounts of drugs passed through there on a weekly basis. They informed the teams about this Adam character and how dangerous he is. The investigators stated this guy was responsible for more than forty deaths they are aware of, and he was a known cop killer.

Tom spoke up, "Take no chances, and under no circumstances are you to approach this guy alone."

One of the team asked if there were any photos of these other players.

Tom said, "We are asking George and John to describe these guys."

Jack spoke up and told both teams, "We don't need heroes. We need captures. We may only get one chance. Do your job and don't try to outthink these guys. If you move from your post, it may give them the crease they need to get away. Once they're gone, we blew our chances to catch them ever again."

One of the team asked when this was going to go down.

Tom spoke up, "In the next few days. We want to make sure we have our ducks in a row before we even think about jumping on these guys."

Jack said, "Make sure you check all of your equipment and make certain everything is ready to go. If there are no more questions, we have to get these guys with a sketch artist to get some descriptions."

Jack and Tom left the room to go back to John and George.

Jack and Tom went back into the interrogation room where George and John were waiting. Jack asked if they would sit with a sketch artist to identify Adam and Kevin. Both of the men looked at Jack and said, "We've never seen Kevin or William."

Tom asked Jack, "What do we do now?" Tom could see Jack was replaying something in his mind

Then Jack said, "Heather. She saw him." Jack told an officer to go to Heather's house and bring her back to sit with the artist.

Tom told one of his men to go with this officer.

Jack said, "If she gives you any grief, arrest her."

The officer and one SBI investigator left, bound for Heather's house.

Once the officer and the SBI investigator arrived at Heather's, they both went to the door and rang the doorbell several times, but there was no answer. The officer called Jack and told him they were at the residence, but there was no one there. The officer asked for further instructions and was told to sit on the house until someone showed up. When Jack got off the phone, he told Tom what he had been told by the officer so he left them to wait it out for Heather.

Back at the station, Jack and Tom were having a discussion regarding the potential leak in the department. Jack decided to just simply sit each member of his team down and have them take a lie detector test and ask them one question, "Have you ever disclosed information about anyone or anything regarding this case to another person outside of this department?"

Tom agreed that was the way to handle the potential leak. Jack called in a polygraph examiner and then announced to everyone on his team they were being required to take this test as he and the SBI want to prove no one on this team leaked information regarding this case. Jack asked if there was anyone who was not comfortable taking this test. A couple of the team members were reluctant and sort of insulted, stating they had given this team everything, and this was like a slap in the face to question their commitment.

Jack just said, "I want to prove our team is solid."

When the polygraph examiner arrived from the SBI office, Jack had him set his equipment in his office for security of the exam. One by one, the investigators started taking the test and then went back to the duties they were doing before. At the end of the testing, one of the investigators asked Jack if he had taken his test?

Jack replied, "I know I didn't leak anything. But you're right, I'll take it also."

At the end of the testing, the examiner asked Jack to come back in. The examiner told Jack everyone passed including himself. Jack thanked the examiner and then called Tom into his office.

Jack advised Tom the whole team had passed, and he sat back in his chair. He thought the only other people who had direct access to this information were the ADA, the DA, the US attorney, and the people who transcribed the interviews.

Tom said, "It certainly wouldn't have been the government's attorneys."

Jack said, "And John's attorney. If Kevin had his hooks into John's attorney, he could have told them everything, and the only reason they didn't kill John was they didn't know where he was."

Tom commented, "I'd bet you're right."

Jack went back to the cell where John and George were and asked John, "What was the name of the attorney you had?"

John told Jack the name.

Jack asked John how he came about using this guy.

John said, "I got the name when I started working with these guys and was told if I ever got pinched, I should call this attorney."

"So when you got released, did you speak to this attorney anymore?"

"No. I was just glad to get out. When the lady ADA told me I could go, I just took off."

Jack asked if he spoke to anyone working for Kevin after he got out, and he said he didn't. He asked John for the attorney's telephone number, and John gave it to him.

Jack questioned how he got up with George.

John answered, "I knew my best bet was to grab some clothes and get lost. So I went up to George's so no one would know where I was."

Tom looked at George and asked if he spoke to Kevin or anyone working with him.

George just said, "No. The only time I hear from him is if he needs something."

Tom asked how Kevin got his car for the pickup.

"He must have come by while John and I were gone on an errand with some friend's of ours. He knew I left the keys in the floor under the mat so he just took it, I guess, and used it to pick up the drugs. Now it all makes sense he wanted me to get caught."

Jack said, "Nice family."

Tom added, "By the way, what errand were you guys running?"

John answered, "We settled some old debts and went back to George's."

Jack spoke up to John, "By the way, I heard from the medical examiner's office, you're not the father."

"I knew that already."

Jack told them to sit tight, and he'd be back. He called the attorney John mentioned and told him he needed to come down to the station regarding some paperwork he needed to sign. The attorney said he would be there tomorrow. Jack, Tom, and the teams decided to go home for the night but left guards with John and George.

On Thursday morning, October 24, Detective Jack Williams awakened, knowing this day was going to be one of the days in his career that will define who he is as an investigator. Jack left earlier than normal, headed for his office, and stopped by to pick up some fast food. When Jack arrived at his office, he began working on his strategy to intercept the drug drop without Kevin or Fred being aware they were being had. The one issue he had was how they were going to pull off capturing Adam since they didn't know where he was during the day. Jack knew he was nearby since the videos were shot in the area of the school that Allison attended. Jack also kept thinking about something John had mentioned regarding Kevin always being in Charlotte when this drug drop was being made.

Tom came into Jack's office about that time, and the two men sat down to bounce ideas off one another. Jack was hoping that when John's lawyer came in today, he would be willing to shed some light on these unanswered questions. The two investigators went in to question John and George a little more about the videos and the drug drops.

Jack and Tom came into the interview room and asked John if he knew where these videos of Allison were shot. John said he didn't know. Jack asked if there were any places in the area that John or George knew where someone like Adam would have felt comfortable enough to do that kind of thing. George stated that Adam could have been anywhere around here. Jack asked if either one of them knew the girl in the video with Allison. George responded he had seen her before but was unsure where.

John's attorney arrived at the station and came into Jack's office. Jack asked him to come in and have a seat, and he would get the paperwork he needed him to sign.

While Jack was gone, Tom introduced himself and began asking the attorney. He asked how he became involved with John.

The attorney said, "He was hired to work on behalf of some friends of John's."

Tom asked the names of those friends.

The attorney stated he was not at liberty to discuss the friend's names with him.

Tom then stated, "When I introduced myself, I neglected to mention I am with the SBI."

The attorney remarked, "I have nothing to say."

Then Tom showed the attorney the girl's photo from the video with Allison and asked him if he knew this girl.

The attorney looked at the photo and asked Tom where he got it.

"She is a person of interest in a case we are working on. You know her. I can tell by the look on your face."

The attorney stated she is his daughter.

Tom asked, "Your daughter?"

The attorney asked where they got the photo, and Tom told him she was involved in the disappearance and death of Allison Tuttle.

The attorney remarked, "She can't be involved in this thing. She was taken away from me when I told these people I wouldn't work for them."

Tom asked when this happened, and the attorney stated right after this guy named Adam got involved with his clients.

Tom said, "Kevin Michaels."

"You know about Kevin?"

"We know a lot more than you think we do, and we know you told Kevin about John and Chuck speaking to us, so therefore, you are involved in their deaths also."

The attorney stated he had nothing to do with that.

Tom said, "So you know they were killed?"

"I just told Kevin what he wanted to know." He then said that he wanted a deal in exchange for his testimony, and the cops have to get his daughter back.

Tom said, "That's up to you and what you tell us about these people."

The attorney stated he needed to be protected from these people. "These people are stone cold killers. They will issue a hit for me when they don't hear from me today. They knew I was coming here to speak to Jack, but I told them it was just some paperwork I needed to sign."

Jack reentered the room about that time. Tom informed him how this attorney got involved with Kevin and Adam. He told Jack about the situation thus far and the attorney had given up both John and Chuck to Kevin.

Jack asked, "So you admit to telling Kevin everything so he would kill them both?"

The attorney answered, "I never meant for them to be killed, but if I didn't give these guys the information they wanted, they would kill my daughter."

Jack asked about the drug deals and drops.

"I knew what they were doing, and it was my job to keep them out of trouble legally."

"Where were these videos shot?

"I have no idea. This was something Kevin wasn't into before this Adam and William showed up. Kevin was and is into drugs, and he uses people to make these drops and pickups, and if they get pinched I try to help them out. If they are a pain in the ass, he just got me to get them released and they take care of them."

Tom clarified, "You mean they kill these people?"

The attorney stated he told Kevin he didn't want to know what happened to these people.

"But you know they were going to kill them when they get out."

The attorney just shrugged his shoulders.

Jack left the room and came back. He asked the attorney to look at the door, and in walked John. The attorney looked like he had seen a ghost.

John said, "You set me up to get killed?"

The attorney told John, "You knew what might happen to you if you talked to the police."

"And you should have known if I ever got pinched again, I'd tell them everything. The girl in the video is his daughter, and he knew what she was doing. He got paid for his daughter's participation in the videos. Fred told me he was the one who wanted his daughter to pose in the videos so he could make money off her looks and ass. He said it was about time she paid him back for the money he spent on her looks."

Tom asked the attorney, "You gave your daughter to these guys just to make money off her? You're nothing but a pimp. And you're a poor excuse for a father." Tom continued, "There goes your deal, counselor."

The attorney spoke, "I can give you all of these guys and a lot more."

Jack whispered something to Tom and then headed out of the office with John.

Jack placed John and George in different interview rooms. Tom began leaning on the attorney to get more information about his lying to the police with regards to his daughter being held by the criminals, but in actuality being placed there by her father. Tom told the attorney that he had just been proven to be a liar by the statement John made. While the two of them talked, Jack was speaking with John.

Jack told John that he obviously knew a lot more than he had shared with us thus far. John stated he was afraid of what these thugs might do to him if he divulged any information that could be used against them. Jack then said, "John, you're up to your eyeballs in this, and there is no way they are giving you a pass. You either talk to me, or if you don't need our help, we'll release you back onto the street. You've got five minutes to think about it, and if Tom has what we need from your attorney in the meantime, we'll release you anyway."

Jack started out of the room when John said, "Where do you want me to start?"

Jack said, "I'll be right back."

Tom got a full statement from the attorney, complete with details of the entire criminal empire, and how everything worked as far as he knew. During his accounting of the business, the attorney also confessed to knowing about the drug business and where the drugs originated from. The attorney also gave up the accounting firm that handled the drug money for Kevin Michaels. He told Tom all about the swag business in Charlotte as well as the video empire, along with the trafficking of the women to pose in these videos.

Tom then asked the attorney who killed Allison, and he stated he had no idea. He added that he was not even aware she had been killed until he heard about it on the television. Tom said, "Are you telling me with a straight face that you had no idea who killed her when you're the mob's attorney?"

The attorney stated he was aware some of the guys had been with her but was never told who killed her.

Tom asked who he thought killed her.

He said, "If it wasn't Adam who killed her, he certainly ordered it to be done. Nothing gets past Adam."

Tom asked for Adam's last name, and the attorney said, "I can honestly say I never knew, and I never asked."

Tom told him to sit tight, and he would be back.

Jack went into the room where George was being held. He walked into the room and said, "George, you have two options. You can talk to me and tell me everything that you know, or I'll cut you loose. And since we are keeping the attorney, I'm sure Kevin won't take any time finding you and killing you."

George looked at Jack and asked him where John was.

Jack said, "He is in another room right now telling us everything."

George asked what was going to happen to him if he tells them what they want to know.

Jack said, "You'll testify against these guys and then be relocated to another part of the country and given a new identity."

"Somewhere warm, I hope."

"I'll be right back."

While Jack went back and picked up the conversation with John, Tom was busy getting more information from George.

Jack told John he was going to record this conversation just so he gets all the information correct. Jack asked John, "Now where were we? Oh, I know. You were going to tell me all about the details of this operation you left out the first time."

John started by saying he was always the kind of person who was loyal up to the time it was going to cost him his freedom or his life.

Jack asked what he could tell him with respect to the drug trafficking.

John answered, "Kevin calls Fred and tells him to get someone to move the packages to or from the drop house. The drop houses are businesses they use that most people would not even suspect of housing drug shipments. Chuck's place was used since Chuck was kind of an idiot, and once he let Fred know he was broke, they had him where they wanted him. Kevin's operation drops stolen jewelry, drugs, or a combination of the two at least once a week and as much as twice a week. The drops and the pickups are made using people who also need money, but also people who can be trusted. The trust part comes when you are tasked with delivering or picking up a certain amount of product. And if you don't have the same amount of product when you get to your destination, they either beat you or a family member of yours. And then they kill someone, either you or your family member. Kevin called it an attention-getter. Fred was just the middle man who usually administered Kevin's punishment."

Jack asked if John knew where the drugs came from.

John said, "The drugs came from the Mexican drug cartel and then into Texas, through tunnels. From Texas, they travel by trucks mixed in with the freight, and they wind up in Charlotte, NC, at an airport hangar facility for private planes. From the hangar in Charlotte, they were transported by vehicle to an abandoned house outside of Elkin, NC, and then distributed to the various drop sites."

Jack asked if he could show them these places, and John confirmed he could. Jack asked about the sex videos, and John said, "Like I've said before, I don't really know a lot about that, other than Adam ran that part of the operation."

"How about the swag that came into Charlotte?"

"The jewelry was stolen all over the country using teams that specifically rob jewelry stores or jewelry couriers. The jewelry was transported via private planes into Charlotte, NC, the main person in charge of each robbery. Usually it was William Thacker who was in charge. The product came in using containers marked Medical Equipment and Radioactive. By doing it that way, no one inspected these packages, and if they x-rayed the containers, the jewelry was actually inside some of the same size and type of containers the real medical equipment was usually shipped in."

Jack was astonished at how defined and exact this operation was. He was in amazement at how much thought had been put into this operation. Jack also knew Kevin couldn't be doing this on his own. He had to be working with someone who had real money and real connections. Jack also thought that in order to get these shipments passed customs, someone had to be paying off customs officials somewhere. Jack told John to sit tight as he wanted to confer with Tom on what he had been told thus far.

Jack went into the room where Tom and George were having their conversation and asked Tom to step outside. Once outside the room, Jack told him all of the things John had said. He also told him he got the whole thing on tape. Jack asked if he was getting anything from George, and Tom shook his head no and then said, "Not yet." Jack told Tom he was going to step back in to see what the attorney has to say. Tom went back into the room where George was.

Jack walked back into the interview room where the attorney was still sitting. He told the attorney that John had told them everything regarding the entire criminal enterprise, and all they needed now was a method to get in touch with Adam. The attorney told Jack he had no idea of how to reach out to Adam. The attorney then said his best bet to get up with Adam was through Fred.

Jack asked where Fred was going to be today and the attorney stated, "He'll be with Kevin today in Charlotte."

Jack asked what time this will be going off.

The attorney stated, "After midnight."

Jack looked at his watch and knew they weren't going to make that deadline since it was already after 11:00 p.m., and they were ninety miles away, so he asked the attorney the next time he could catch up with Fred.

"The next drops would be done on Monday at the local burger joint."

"We will be taking you, John, and George to a holding facility soon to spend the night." Jack left the room.

Jack called the sheriff's department to have the prisoners transported to the Forsyth County jail until morning. Jack made sure he told them these prisoners were to be placed in a maximum security cell block and guarded twenty-four hours a day.

Jack then went back to the holding cell where George and Tom were. He knocked on the door and asked Tom if he was finished with George for the night since the sheriff department was on their way to transport these guys. Tom said he was, and they waited for the transport vehicle. The men were transported, and the investigators went home.

On Friday morning, October 25 Jack was actually excited for the first time since this case began. He was excited for the opportunity to stop these criminals in their tracks and derail this drug train in his town. Jack knew the people being held knew enough about this enterprise to severely cripple this business, but Jack was not satisfied by simply stopping the drugs and swag. Bringing all these thugs to justice was his optimal goal.

Jack called the sheriff's department to have them bring the prisoners back to the station this morning. When Jack arrived at his office, the prisoners were just being brought back as he requested. As they were being unloaded, a vehicle drove by, and shots were fired from the vehicle, striking two of the prisoners as well as one of the deputies. The vehicle took off down the road, going away from the station as Jack and the other SBI agents gave chase in their cruisers. Jack was on the radio reporting shots fired and the call of 213, which meant officer down at the station. Jack and the agents continued to chase until the men in the car were also firing at them. The chase continued for a few miles until the shooters reached a bridge outside of town where officers had set up spike strips. As the eluding vehicle hit the strips, their tires were shredded, and the driver of the vehicle lost control.

As the vehicle skidded off the road, the shooters jumped from the vehicle only to be met with police officers and SBI agents fully armed. A gunfight ensued. The three men from the vehicle were shot upon from all angles until two of the three men had been hit, and the third man surrendered. Medical was called for the two men who were shot during the exchange of gunfire. They were fatally wounded at the scene. The third shooter was arrested and taken to Jack's station for questioning.

Jack called Tom to see how the prisoners were doing and told him the chase ended with two of the shooters being fatally wounded at the scene. Tom told Jack that the attorney was dead and George was severely wounded and rushed to the hospital. The deputy was wounded but would recover. Jack asked about John and was told that he would recover as he was struck only in the forearm. Jack told Tom to be sure the media won't print any of this as it would endanger their other witnesses. Tom agreed.

Jack told Tom, "Well I guess we know now we struck a nerve."

"I'd say so."

Jack said he would be back at the station in just a few minutes.

When Jack arrived back at the station, Tom told him he thought the FBI needed to be called.

Jack told him, "No way. We are not seeing this case this far only to turn this over to those glory seekers. I have been working this case since September 19, and I will not turn it over to anyone. If you want to quit, then quit, but you're not giving my case away."

Tom told Jack he was only thinking of where this case may be going.

"I know where it's going. We are going to find these people and capture them or kill them. Either way, we win. No, let me say that differently, Allison wins."

Tom said, "I'm with you, and my team is with me."

Jack and Tom left for the hospital to pick up John and get him back to their station.

When Jack and Tom arrived at the hospital to pick John up, he was not in very good spirits. John was really upset these guys had tried to kill him after all he had done for them over time. Tom had his men stand guard with weapons drawn as John was lead out to the cruiser. As they drove away, there was an armed escort leading the cruiser with John in it as well as a trailing vehicle with armed SBI agents following closely behind. The group drove directly to the station and placed John in a secured cell, being guarded full-time. Jack and Tom went into the cell and started speaking with John. John said, "So are we going to get these bastards or not?"

Jack said, "You bet we are."

"So what's our next move?"

The three men started having a discussion in private about their plans to capture these criminals.

When Jack and Tom exited the cell, they went into Jack's office with Jack's team and the SBI agents. The group was in the office for more than two hours. When the group came out, Jack called the hospital to see how George was doing. The hospital stated he was in the ICU after coming out of surgery. Jack was told George had suffered a collapsed lung along with having being shot in his torso several times. Jack asked if he was going to be all right and was told his chances were less than 50/50. Jack thanked them for the update and asked to keep him posted. He had also dispatched officers to stand guard over George.

Jack went into the interview room where the third shooter was being held. Jack asked him for his name, and the man stated he didn't have to tell him anything. Jack grabbed the man and jerked him up from his seat. He got right into his face and told him, "You want to play like a big boy, then I'll treat you like a big boy? You killed an officer of the court, and shot two other men one of whom is in intensive care. If they'd give me the okay, I'd put the needle in your arm myself."

The man said, "You're violating my rights."

"You don't have any rights. Not here."

"I want my lawyer."

"Better yet, I'll let you go, and I'll announce to the news media you worked with us and gave up the people you worked for. How about that?"

"You can't do that."

"Wait here while I call the news people."

Jack left when the man said, "Okay, I don't need a lawyer. I'll tell you what I know."

"Let me get a tape recorder and a witness." Jack went to get the recorder and Tom.

When the two men came back into the room, Jack started the recorder and asked the man his name. The man gave his name and his other information. Jack started asking the man about who had hired the other men. The man stated that Joe and Tom, who were fatally shot by the officers, were guys he knew, and they hired him to help them. He thought they were doing a robbery, and then the next thing he knew was the men handed him a gun and told him to fire at these guys when they drove by the station. He said, "I never even fired a shot. Check the gun. There was no way I was shooting at cops. Then when the chase started, I was just along for the ride. I admit I have robbed places for them, but shooting cops, no way, man."

Jack asked where they got the guns, and the man told Jack they already had the guns in the car when they picked him up.

The man said, "I'm used to having a gun for the robberies, but shooting a cop, that's not what I do. That's the gas chamber."

Jack asked about the robberies, and the man gave Jack all the information he knew about, including a robbery that was coming up in Mt. Airy, NC, a town nearby. He asked when the robbery was going down.

The man told Jack it was going down today about 3:00 p.m. since the store was getting a new supply of jewelry about that time.

Jack looked at his watch and asked how he knew for sure this was happening.

The man said, "My brother is one of the robbers, and he told me."

Jack asked how exactly this was going to be done, and the man gave him all of the details. Jack asked how many people were on this robbery today, and the man told him the number. Jack told the man if his information checked out, they might be willing to speak to the DA on his behalf. Jack and Tom left the room to decide how to handle this. The two investigators went into Jack's office with three members of the SBI team and two of Jack's team to plot their strategy. When the team came out of Jack's office, they started getting ready for the robbery in Mt. Airy and got all of the maps and other materials needed to stop any getaway from the jewelry store. Jack went back into John's room to speak with him about the robbery and ask a few questions.

Jack asked John when they did a robbery, what the robbers did with the jewelry once they had done the job. John gave Jack the information and also told them where the people would meet afterward. Jack got a lot of good credible information from John, so they would be prepared to take down the handoff of the stolen jewelry. Jack asked what happened from that point, and John told him that also. Jack thanked him for the information. John asked if he could go along, and Jack stated he was more valuable right where he was since he knew all the details of these robberies. Jack left the room.

Jack, Tom, and the officers left the station bound for Mt. Airy prepared for the upcoming robbery attempt. On the way to the robbery, Jack and the team strategized the whole scenario and thought through every miniscule detail. When the team arrived on sight, they began to set up lookout positions and prepared for the robbers. About 2:55 p.m., the men described to Jack by the third shooter appeared, and two of the men entered the store in ski masks just like it had been described. Jack and the team watched from a distance waiting on the men to exit the store. In three to four minutes, the robbers exited the store as planned and left the area. Jack and his team followed the men from a distance out-of-town.

Other lookout points had been set up, knowing the men would be traveling to a location where the remainder of Jack's team and the other SBI agents were already waiting. Jack was in constant radio contact with the other teams, and everything was ready when the crooks arrived. The robbers drove up to the location previously described by John only to find themselves surrounded by nothing but armed agents and police. After a brief standoff, the men surrendered. Jack told the brother of the man at their station to call Fred and tell him everything went fine just like he was told to do. The man made the call with an armed agent standing by his side, listening to the call with a gun pointed at the man's head.

Fred told the man what a great job they did and to meet him at the drop-off point like always. The robber told Fred he would and hung up the phone. Jack patted him on the head and told him he did a great job for them too. Jack had some of the team's men take the prisoners back to the station while the remainder of the team went on to topple the next domino in this criminal family.

Jack, Tom, and the team went to the next location for the meeting with Fred. Thanks to John, they already knew where this meeting was going to be held, so once again the other portion of the team was waiting for them at this meeting. When Jack and Tom met with John, they got all the information they needed to be able to position members of each team in the meeting locations so as to ambush the men as they met to exchange the stolen items. John knew these meetings were held in public places so not to attract attention to themselves, but in this case these meeting places worked against them since there were so many people present that no one can notice the presence of the officers in unmarked vehicles and plain clothes.

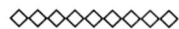

When the man got to the location to meet with Fred, another officer was on the floor of the vehicle to make sure he didn't call Fred and tip him off as to what was happening. When the man pulled up in the parking lot, he got out of the vehicle as planned and carried a shopping bag full of stolen jewelry. The plan was he would meet with Fred and then handoff the shopping bag. When the man handed off the bag to Fred, they found themselves surrounded by Jack's team with loaded guns pointed at them.

Tom told Fred to drop his weapon before he got shot.

Fred stated he didn't have a weapon.

Tom said, "Look on the back of your belt under your coat."

Fred said, "John."

Jack got out of his cruiser and walked up to Fred and said, "Yeah, John." Jack introduced himself to Fred and then said, "Nice to finally meet you." The investigators then took him into custody for transport to the station.

On the way back to the station, Jack told Fred, "By the way, John is not dead, obviously. The next time you tell your goons to kill someone, you might want to make sure you're not using the Three Stooges to carry out your plan."

Fred said, "I didn't order the hit on John."

"Really? That's not the word on the street."

"When John did not get back in touch with us after he was seen talking to you guys, it was only natural he was working with you. People who work with the police are like rats, and when you have a rat, you call an exterminator." He continued, "I'm not talking anymore until I see my attorney."

Jack laughed and then said, "I hope you brought your Ouija board since those idiots killed your attorney. By the way, one of those idiots is still alive, and the other two joined your attorney. They're dead too. When we get to the station, you guys can have a family reunion."

"I still want an attorney."

"No problem."

When Jack and the others got back to the station, they brought Fred inside. When they entered the building, Fred saw John and said, "You could have been rich, but no, you had to run your mouth."

John said, "You tried to have me killed. Just seeing you in handcuffs makes my day."

"There's no way I am going to flip Kevin."

"I counted on that already."

The investigators had searched Fred, and they had his cell phone and the gun he had on him when they arrested him.

Jack had the forensic team come over and got a mouth swab to see if he was the baby's father. While they waited on the results from the swab, they asked Fred if he wanted to give them a statement. But he wouldn't speak.

Jack called the DA's office and told them they had arrested the suspect from the Mt. Airy robbery, and the other two were dead. They also told the DA that they had Fred in custody and were waiting for his fingerprints to get his full identity. While the DA's office was on the phone, they told them the attorney was also dead, and George and John had been shot. Jack explained that George was in critical condition in the ICU while John was there at the station after being treated at the hospital and released. Jack got off the phone with the DA when the forensic specialist came into his office. The results were negative for Fred's DNA as being the father of Allison's baby.

Jack walked over to speak to Tom and John again in private to plot their next move. Tom had an idea of how to bring Kevin out of hiding, and then Jack expressed his thoughts. John scratched his head and then said, "What if——"

Both Tom and Jack thought that would be the perfect scenario to bring Kevin to them.

Someone from the public defender's office showed up to speak with Fred. Fred was really upset to see this public defender and refused to speak to him. He said, "I want a real attorney, not this wannabe."

Jack told him, "The law says you have to have legal representation. It doesn't say it has to be good representation."

"I'm entitled to a phone call."

"And you shall have it. What number do you want to call, and we'll dial it for you."

"I'm not giving you the number."

"It's my phone, and if you don't give us the number, we're not making the call."

Fred just sat back down and wouldn't speak again. While this exchange was going on, the results were in on Fred's fingerprint results. His fingerprints came back to Frederick Antonio Benardo, a.k.a. Freddy Bernardo, a.k.a. Fast Freddy, a.k.a. Tony Bernardo. He was from New Jersey and was linked to the Bernardo crime family. He had been in prison for armed robbery, murder, manslaughter, and other smaller offenses. Now Jack knew where some of this money was coming from.

While all of this was going on, John had called Kevin directly from Fred's phone. John told Kevin he had intercepted the jewelry from the heist in Mt. Airy, and he had gone to the meeting places and got Fred. John stated he was not very happy that Fred tried to have him killed. Kevin stated that he was very disappointed at Fred's performance as of late, and he had always wanted John to take over that position except for the fact he was working with the police. John told him he had gotten pinched by the police and was making them think he was giving them good information. John said, "Have they raided any of the drop sites or the drop houses? Have they arrested you or Adam? I just want my share, and if you won't meet me, I'm going to take it out of what I've collected from Fred. By the way, in the trunk of Fred's car were about fourteen little packages I could also take if you don't want them."

Kevin said, "How do I know you're not going to set me up?"

"You don't, but if I was going to set you up, I could have sent them to the hangar anytime. You and I both know what goes on there."

"So what is it you want?"

"I want my money for what you owe me."

"So how do we make this happen without me getting arrested? You're probably at the station right now."

"You want to speak to Fred?"

"No. When and where."

"Well, since I know you are going to have me run from place to place so you can make sure I'm not followed, why don't we start at the burger joint, and then you can send me running from there?"

"You know me too well."

"I'll be there tomorrow morning 10:00 a.m."

"Okay."

John got off the phone and he, Jack, and Tom went into Jack's office to talk about the meeting tomorrow. Jack asked why he didn't have Kevin meet him right now.

John answered, "If I had done that, he would have smelled something was wrong. Kevin doesn't do anything on the spur of the moment. He moves cautiously and carefully. By doing it in the morning, it gives him plenty of time to stake out the parking lot and to have other people watching me. All he is going to do is run me around with people watching me." With that, John said he needed to not be at the station.

Jack asked where John was going, and he told them he will be staying with a friend where he knew he would be safe. Tom and Jack reluctantly agreed and advised him that they would be watching as well. John also took a car used by one of Jack's team so he would have a vehicle that Kevin wouldn't recognize. What John didn't know was while he was there chatting with Jack and Tom, they had a tracking device installed on John's new ride. John had the jewelry with him and the packages they had actually found in the trunk of Fred's car. John told Jack that Kevin was going to expect him to have a gun, and he needed something with no records. Tom said he was not in favor of taking a gun, but John convinced them that if he didn't have a gun, then how he would have gotten Fred to come with him? After a few minutes, Jack agreed. Jack told John, "If you're scamming me, we will find you."

After John left the station, the two investigators started talking about the risk they were taking. Jack said, "If this blows up, blame me."

Tom said, "We have to be on top of this all the way."

"Look on the bright side. We can still bust the operation in Charlotte."

"If it exists. All we have is John's word."

"Well, he has been instrumental in picking up these other guys."

"And thus far, his information had been right on track."

"Let's trust him and see what happens." Jack continued, "Let's look at how we're going to get to him if and when he needs our help."

Tom stated they have a tracking device on the vehicle so they will know where the vehicle is at all times. Jack and Tom decided to go home and get some rest for what may prove to be a long day tomorrow.

An All-American Girl

On Saturday morning, October 26, Jack began the day as he usually does, except he had a handheld toy showing the tracking information as to John's whereabouts. Jack looked at the scanner to see where John had been during the night. The scanner showed John had gone to a restaurant to get some food and then to an address and spent the remainder of the night there, or at least the car was there. Jack couldn't resist the temptation to ride by just to see if the car was at this location. Another part of Jack's brain was thinking he would hate to be followed and lead someone right to John. He decided, since he still would have no way of knowing if John was inside, to go to the office.

When Jack arrived at his office, Tom was already there with breakfast for everyone on the team. Jack was pleasantly surprised, and he told Tom according to the tracking device that the car John had was at a stationary location all night. Tom stated he was glad John had done the right thing and resisted going out anywhere. The men all sat in the station waiting for John's first stop to begin at 10:00 a.m.

When John was at the burger joint precisely at the correct time, he received a call from Kevin as scheduled. Kevin told him to go to King and wait at the diner there. When John arrived at that diner, he got another call from Kevin who told him to go to the parking lot outside of Walmart and park near the Goodwill Donation trailer and wait. Jack had different units watching John, so Kevin would not be suspicious of any one vehicle. This continued until about 1:00 p.m. when John arrived at the parking lot behind the pizza place on University Parkway close to Big Lots and waited. John sat patiently in the car until the phone rang again about 1:40 p.m. John was thinking that Kevin will not call after forty minutes. When John answered the phone, Kevin told John to meet him at the Old Man's Place. John started the car and headed off going north on University Parkway and then turned left on Highway 65 going west. John was on Highway 65 west until he got to Bethania and then turned toward Clemmons/Lewisville.

Jack's men followed John until he got to an intersection and went west on Yadkinville Road. The investigators were following John and radioing their location. John turned in at an old farmhouse outside of Lewisville, which was a very deserted area so the team had to break away from following John and split off down dirt roads in the area so they didn't tip off Kevin. The investigators then had to trek their way through the woods until they got close to John's location.

Jack warned everyone not to get burned, or this guy would just kill John and take off. Jack and Tom went a different way to try and outflank Kevin. John pulled down the road until he got to an outbuilding that was falling down, where another vehicle was waiting. John got out of the car when he came to a stop and just stood there next to the car.

Another man got out of the other car and pointed a gun at John, which made Jack very nervous. Jack and Tom had a listening device with them so they could hear what John and Kevin were talking about.

The man told John to open his jacket so he could see his sides and then to raise the coat up and turn around so he could see his back and his belt. The man then had John remove the coat and drop it to the ground. The man told John to raise his pant legs so he could see his ankles to make sure he didn't have a gun. The man then asked John where the gun was, and John replied it was in his coat. The man then walked over to John and picked up the coat. The gun was found in the coat just like John had said. The man raised the gun high enough for a second man to see from the car.

Jack and Tom watched as a third man got out of the backseat from the other vehicle. The third man was a large man with a camel hair coat on and lots of jewelry on his hands. He walked very slowly closer to where John was. The man walked right up to John and got very close to John's face, stared at him, and said, "Good to see you again. Where is my product?"

John said, "In the car."

The man nodded and told the other man to get the drugs and the jewelry.

The other man went to the car John drove and started searching the backseat and floor.

John said, "Do I look stupid, Kevin? You taught me well. I left a package containing the drugs and the jewelry with a friend of mine and told him if he doesn't hear from me today by 7:00 p.m., he is to take that package to Detective Jack Williams."

Kevin said, "Why should I believe you?"

"You can't afford not to believe in me. If I don't call, my friend, the package that Jack gets has everything I know about you and Adam, along with photos of you at the hangar with the containers. Nice photos by the way, really great color. I also included dates and times when other robberies occurred. The one thing they will like even better is just for old-time sake. I threw a list of the video sales so they could track Adam too. I think it's about time Adam meet Detective Williams, don't you? Like I said, you taught me well."

Kevin smiled and said, "You always were a pain, I see nothing's changed. So you want to get in all the way?"

"Yes. You are one who makes all the money, and I'm smart enough to take over and be your right-hand man."

"Where's Fred?"

"Does it matter?"

"Not really, I assume you killed him."

"Wouldn't you? The jerk tried to have me killed."

Kevin asked John where he had buried the body.

John said, "A spot you used before."

Kevin nodded and then said, "Nice."

Kevin scratched the side of his cheek and said, "When can I get my product?"

"So what about my deal?"

"I'll have to run this by Adam first."

"No problem. I'll have Fred's phone, and you can call me when you have his okay."

Kevin said, "I don't need his okay, but I want to see what he thinks about this deal."

"Call him now." John knew if Kevin called Adam, the police would be able to trace the call.

Kevin stood there a minute and then said, "You're in. Now when can I get my product?"

"As soon as I get the money I'm owed."

Kevin nodded he was okay with that.

The men shook hands and were getting ready to leave the area.

Jack still had Kevin in his gunsight when one of the agents tripped over a branch trying to get back to his cruiser.

Kevin looked right at John and said, "You set me up," and reached for his gun.

Jack shot Kevin in the shoulder. Tom then shot the driver with his rifle he had trained on him the entire time. The teams moved in immediately to take the men into custody. Jack called for EMS since both Kevin and the driver had been shot.

While they waited for the EMS, Jack spoke to Kevin and told him they heard the whole conversation and had everything on tape.

Kevin looked at John and said, "I'll get you when I get out."

Jack spoke up and said, "The thing is, Kevin, you're never getting out."

Tom searched Kevin's car when he came over to John and said, "You're a lucky man. I found a one-way ticket to St. Thomas in the trunk of Kevin's car along with ten million dollars in cash. He was planning on killing you before you left here today."

Kevin said, "Business is business, and Christmas is Christmas. I try to never leave loose ends."

When the EMS arrived, Jack also told them to get DNA from Kevin and send it to the crime lab.

Jack asked Kevin, "The one thing I don't understand is why you had to kill Allison Tuttle. You gave her the diamond earrings she wore."

Kevin said, "I never said I killed her."

Jack asked, "Did you?"

Kevin just smiled and said, "She wanted something more from me than I was willing to give."

Jack asked again if he killed her, but Kevin would not respond. Jack looked confused and asked Tom if he had just admitted he murdered Allison. Tom said, "I don't know."

Tom and Jack sent several officers with the EMS team and told them not to let Kevin out of their sight for any reason. Jack also told them not to transport Kevin from the hospital without SWAT being present.

Once Kevin's injuries were treated, he was transported to the Forsyth County jail with the support of SWAT where he is awaiting trial for the murder of Allison Tuttle along with 140 counts of drug trafficking, intimidation of a witness, communicating threats, and other various charges.

Adam, William Thacker, and Tony Bolero remain at large.

The morning after Kevin was arrested, Detective Jack Williams rang the doorbell at the Tuttle's house, and Jennifer answered the door.

Jack looked right at her and said, "You never told me you had another son."